CHASING A CURE

A Zombie Novel

RM Hamrick

This is a work of fiction. Names, characters, businesses, places, events and incidents are either the products of the author's imagination or used in a fictitious manner. Any resemblance to actual persons, living or dead, or actual events is purely coincidental.

Cover design by Covers by Christian
Editing by Sticks and Stones Editing

ISBN-13: 978-1973737377
ISBN-10: 197373737X

To all the runners.
In case of apocalypse, we'll be best able to run away from zombies.

To Mom + Dad,
Thank you for making
this possible. Love,
RMH

CHAPTER ONE

Audra looked past the makeshift shelter to the soft drops of rain. She knew it could devolve into a sudden storm and bring down their hovel of fence sections and tree branches. But for now, it was almost pleasant. Audra imagined the place would not be much smaller with a collapse. The three inhabitants already crawled on top of each other. For a moment, she took a deep breath and appreciated the structure's ability to hide them from the biters, and the rain's patter to mask her mom's quiet groans and her older sister's whimpers.

Now was as good a time as any.

In the isolated wood with no biters in sight, Audra turned her attention to her mother's leg. The pant leg had been cut to her high thigh weeks ago to dress the wound. It had been redressed several times now, but it was still difficult to separate the flesh from the dressing. Her dad's quick actions had stopped the bleeding at the scene, but now Audra wished upon everything it would bleed again. Instead a smelly, hot ooze had taken over. Dad was gone now, but Audra did not need his life's wisdom to know the same incident that took his life would also take her mom's.

As Audra cleaned the wound, her dark auburn hair fell over her green eyes, despite its sticky dirt and grease. Her mom allowed her to help today. A few days before, she had sent them away, in order to cut out the dying flesh and drain the wound herself. She had wanted to protect her twelve- and sixteen-year-old girls from the harshness of near-death, but Audra would have been able to handle it. She was always stoic, even before all this happened, never crying over scraped knees or unfair treatment. But still, her mother had insisted that she did not need to cut dead tissue from a wound. Now Belinda lay in her mother's arms, positioned away from the injured leg. The daughter gazed into her mother's face, searching for comfort. She didn't notice how warm her mother had gotten or what was unfolding around her.

It wasn't even a bite.

It was just an infected cut, maybe from a poor machete swing. No one remembered in the frenzy of the attack. And wandering through the woods with no supplies, it was impossible to keep it clean. The cleaning and re-wrapping were a futile effort. No sterile sutures or bandaging, no antibiotics. They did not even have clean water. Audra assessed the wound one last time and decided. She met her mom's eyes. The infection had not taken the grit from them. She nodded her agreement above Belinda's head, out of her sight. It was not supposed to happen this way. As a family, they had survived the initial outbreak. They were surviving. Their days had become routine, normal. Audra packed without a word to her sister, careful to hide items of comfort behind for their mother.

Now a new normal would take over.

It was not long before Belinda noticed the change in routine and her panic floated to the surface. It was never far. The mom held her oldest tight and gave her small kisses on her forehead. Belinda's cries only got louder. Once again, she looked to her youngest.

"Take care of your sister. You're all she has left."

Audra nodded her promise and continued packing supplies. The rain might stop soon and they would need plenty of time to set up camp before night fell.

A noise stopped her rummaging.

Belinda whimpered and her mother hushed her. Outside, one crept past, none the wiser of the lean-to in the rain. Audra watched from inside. The zombie's jaw, unhinged and off-center, gathered water. The skin on his face was swollen and distended from his time spent exposed. His pant leg caught on a root as he walked past. With his leg dragging, the mirror image of her mother soon wandering the woods came unbidden.

* * *

"Look, dude. I saw him first," Audra shouted into the woods toward the man.

She caught side glimpses of him through the brush. He was easy to spot with a large green backpack slowing him down. Her first pursuer was directly behind her. All six feet of him seemed to lean forward from his ankles to reach her. A blood stain darkened the arm of his business suit. He was a perfect specimen aside from a small tear at the corner of his mouth. Nothing a few stitches couldn't fix. His shambling chase did not worry Audra. The man running alongside them in the isolated woods did. She stole another glance and tried to size him up. She did not recognize him or know his intentions, but he was trying to cut them off.

This newcomer could foil her plan to take off around a hill bend and come back behind the zom to tag him with her biometric reader. He could cut over to snipe her find. Whoever scanned first received Finder's Rights. All was fair in the game of tagging, but that didn't mean she wouldn't be pissed. This was her find.

She would at least make it more difficult for him.

Audra picked up speed and teased her zom to follow. Soon they were moving at a quick pace. She could hear both men in the heavy woods laboring to keep up, tripping, and bumbling. The backpack was too big for chases through the branches and brambles. No wonder he was trying to poach her find. And this was a good one. He looked like he came from a wealthy family. Someone could be looking for him.

She heard a big "Oomph" followed by a crash. One of them had tripped hard. Audra glanced back again. The zombie, nonplussed by the sound, still focused on her backside. With his visual and olfactory senses locked in, hearing became less important. She veered to the left, away from their fallen pursuer. A minute later she looked back and saw no signs of him. She noticed her zombie's shoe had fallen off. His black-socked foot stomped over rocks and sticks.

She did not want to damage the goods.

She took off into a sprint and disappeared behind a big oak tree. The zombie grunted in anger and continued in his same direction, not having enough reasoning skills to change his mind. As he passed the oak tree, Audra was ready with her silver handheld reader. She scraped the sharp comb along the back of the neck, above his falling suit collar. He turned, and she fended him off as she retracted the comb into the device for analysis.

She elbowed him. When he twisted around, she kicked the back of his knee. He fell to the ground, face smashing first.

She sat on his back. Her foot contacted the back of his head, more to muffle his angry noises than to keep herself safe. She pulled out a prickly pear pad from her bag to munch on while she waited for the reader to analyze the DNA.

BING, BING came the beautiful sound, the sound of money.

"Let's see who wants to pay for you, my friend," she directed toward the zom underfoot with a renewed smile on her face. The thought of his torn mouth flashed into her mind. She should not push his face too far into the ground. He was worth money now, and the better his physical condition, the better the payout.

The readout display had text stats on her find. Every person's DNA had been cataloged for almost 25 years before the outbreak. And now that information was used to determine if your corpse body would be awakened or if you would continue to roam the countryside, a remnant of your former self. Today was her and Randolph Ludington's lucky day.

Name: Randolph Ludington
Gender: Male
DOB: 5/29/2043
Status: Deposit paid

There were three potential status findings: No Inquiries, Inquired, and Deposit Paid. A deposit started the wake-up process - if, by process, you meant negotiation.

Audra punched the FOUND key as she settled onto her zombie seat. The usual survey followed, documenting body condition, difficulty of capture (in this case, already captured), and distance from Lysent headquarters. Audra typed in the answers as she chewed on the end of the cactus pad. It was her last prepared one. She would have to be on the lookout for more.

It would take a while for Lysent to contact the depositor and negotiate a price. She surveyed her surroundings. Was the stranger still lurking around to snatch her zom? Technically now that she had pressed FOUND, she was the only one entitled to the corporation's payout through Finder's Rights. But there were always loopholes. If poaching was enticing earlier, it was now even more tempting. Any zombie with 'No Inquiry' status would be left to roam with a yellow serial tag on his ear. Audra's attachment to him showed his value. It was time to find a camp, away from here and close to water.

She leaned forward, moving from her rear to a kneel, pushing each knee into a shoulder. She inched the bartered handmade leather mask over his face, taking care that her fingers did not slip near his teeth. One bite and she would be infected and wandering the woods, too. Some taggers removed the teeth, and the awakened person would be given dentures afterward. Keeping him intact would yield a better payout. Audra tightened the lacing of the mask and finished with a Carrick bend like her father had taught her. She got off the zom's back and pulled up on the knot to bring him to his knees. The mask had an eye slot, but for now, she threw a small cloth sack over his head to block his view and calm him. He could still smell her though. The mask muffled his noises, but his arms reached wide to find the source of the smell. She grabbed and bound his hands in front of him with soft, wide cloth to prevent injuries to his limbs. Prices dropped fast with amputations. The cure could not regrow limbs or extensive tissue. She hitched a long lead to his binding.

With his arms bound and his nickname chosen, Audra pulled the cloth sack off Randy's head so they could walk without stumbling - too much.

Audra knew the Georgia woods, or what was left of Georgia. Really, the only townships this far south belonged to Lysent. The goal was a secluded spot where she could start a fire and have a nice campsite without being found by others. If she was stuck with Randy for a few days, at least she should be able to enjoy it. Sometimes she would travel with a zom toward Lysent before a negotiation's end, but the date of Randy's deposit was old. His family's circumstances may have changed. She wanted to be out here if his deal did not go through. The land near Lysent was already well hunted. Besides, Randy was so demure, she could handle at least one more zombie if she found it in time. She was sure Randy would love another travel buddy.

Audra was stuck working for Lysent. Most of the time, money never exchanged hands between her and the corporation. She had indebted herself to them as an indentured tagger. She could ask for a payout when she needed to buy items, but it lengthened her employment. It seemed like a never-ending battle anyway, as she incurred more debt each day.

Audra tried not to think about it.

Randy grunted as he caught on a high root that Audra had missed. The rope gave a quick tug and Audra jumped ahead to miss his fall. Over the last two years, she had become adept at feeling the tautness and looseness of her lead. His cadence, the vibrations of his steps, his unfortunate scent all gave her information.

They walked eight miles plus another two to find a good

camping spot. Audra controlled most of the conversation. She tried to guess Randy's occupation before his unfortunate accident (Were you a stockbroker, Randy?). His suit gave away that he was in the initial outbreak. Once people learned there was a disease sweeping the country that turned you into a cannibal, they stopped donning suits. She complimented him on his obviously successful efforts to stay in one piece. Most of his colleagues had since decomposed beyond what was salvageable.

The conversation ended for a while as Audra set up camp. She tied him to a thick sapling, threw down her pop up tent, and gathered wood for her fire. As she roasted her found hickory nuts, the sun set behind the trees and the woods darkened. She set her eyes on the fire, but kept her ears on the forest past the fire's crackle and Randy's shuffling. Was someone out there? Another zombie would be nice, another tagger would be bad, to wildlife she was neutral. Any large predators had plenty to eat with the zombies walking around. They were easier prey.

"I wish we had marshmallows to toast, Randy. Do you remember marshmallows?"

Zombies required nutrition, but marshmallows wouldn't cut it. The virus stimulated the brain's hunger response only toward non-infected humans, as a way for it to spread through the bodily fluid exchange of bites. The virus attacked higher brain structures, leaving parts responsible for survival and basic movement functioning. The heart pumped. The lungs breathed. And the five senses seemed intact. But it all happened at a slower pace. The slowed breathing and heart rate diminished the amount of oxygen delivered to the body. The bodies began to look dead, sagging and decaying. With their bodies running at such low capacities, it took an extended amount of time for them to starve to death, over a year in fact by Lysent's estimations. The cure couldn't awaken the actual dead, only those infected with the virus.

When had Randy eaten last? She wondered.

*   *   *

"I wish we had marshmallows to toast," said Audra.

Her voice tried to lighten the mood, but her eyes remained dark staring at the sparks coming off the fire. Belinda hunched over the fire Audra had built, crying like she had for the last three days. Her blond hair clung to her face with the wetness, her peripheral vision lost. Audra did not know you could shed that many tears and still maintain your eyeballs' shape. At least the tears streamed without noisy broadcast, only an odd sniffle timed with footfalls as she followed Audra through the woods. Audra offered her water again to compensate for the continual dehydration from her eyes. Belinda swiped and yanked the bottle from her hand. Her eyes like wet ice, flashed with anger.

"How can you even think about sweets?"

Audra ignored the comment. She had ignored a lot of comments in the three days since they had left their mother. Despite that having been their mom's idea and insistence, Belinda blamed Audra. She had forced Belinda to desert her mother and now they were alone. Audra did not cry, and that angered Belinda, but Belinda did enough crying for the both of them. Someone needed to stay aware and her mom had chosen her.

No reason to set up their crappy makeshift tarp-on-sticks. There would be no rain tonight. Audra took all their soft things and put them on the ground in a pile. The navy sky filled with stars and planets. That was one of the few good things to emerge from the loss of the modern world. No more light pollution.

Satellites flew through the dome of visible space. They kept their orbits, useless and irrelevant.

Belinda moved from her spot and curled up against Audra. Her head felt heavy on Audra's chest. Her hair tickled her nose. Her body felt warm and soft.

"I love you, Audra."

The words were whispered into her chest, almost inaudible. It was hard to stay mad at her. Her blue eyes would go wide at any sign of trouble and her body would freeze. She bubbled with emotion and fear. The new world only amplified these characteristics. But it was easy to care for the beautiful girl with the sweet smile. Audra often forgot herself that Belinda was four years her senior. She cared for her like a younger sister.

"I love you," Audra repeated as she closed her eyes and enjoyed the brief reprieve.

* * *

Audra's eyes opened with the dawn. She could not imagine sleeping through the deafening roar of the birds. Even the late ones woke with the sun. Audra peeled herself off the floor and threw her pack outside. She broke down the tent and put it in her bag. Even having a "camp" meant being ready to run at a moment's notice. It had taken months to find a tent, and she was not about to abandon it because of some damn zom herd. She said good morning to Randy and asked if he would like any coffee. He declined, which was a good thing because she had none. Coffee beans were expensive as hell. And not fresh. Audra disliked coffee as a child before the outbreak. She had not grown to enjoy it as an expensive, watered-down luxury.

Audra pulled her food down from where she had hung it from a tree. Despite plenty of slow-moving flesh, bears still went for easy picnic baskets. She opened the pack and did the math. Math and food had become second nature to her. She knew how much she needed to eat each day to be comfortable. She did not double-check her math when she came up short. She was always short, but she did not need much today - no running if she could help it. She decided to forage for breakfast.

She told Randy to guard their empty camp spot. On second thought, she dropped him to the ground and bound his feet. She did not want him making too much noise with another runner around. Pain in the ass Randy. He was such a good walker though. She secured his limbs and let him rest on the forest floor. She pulled on her pack and began exploring.

The forest exploded with nuts and berries with the late spring weather. She collected her favorites along with some greens. She snacked on them as she continued around the area, looking for signs of another zombie or human. A mile out, she saw signs of trampling as if a zom or a careless hiker had passed through… or both. The question was soon answered.

The unmistakable "Rawnrerr" of a zombie and the grunts of a human echoed through the forest. The human sounded like he was struggling. Audra deftly maneuvered downhill to the source of the noises. Her scent was upwind, but Audra would have been surprised if anyone noticed. They were busy.

Audra could mind her own business, but if the human failed, there would be two zombies to check out and cash in. And even if he did not, Audra wanted to know who was so close to her campsite. It was probably that idiot trying to kidnap Randy from her. Audra already felt annoyed, and she had not even met him yet.

She got to the bottom of the hill and there he was, big-green-pack guy. He had a stick in one hand, stabbing at the zombie, putting holes in the merchandise. In the other, he had a brand new, shiny reader. Any safe distance he gained with the stick thwarted his ability to retrieve a DNA sample.

The zombie was much more decomposed than her Randy and getting worse by the minute. The big-green-pack guy continued to yell, causing the zombie to flail about and further the damage. He did not know he was within arm's reach of a woman standing behind him.

"Wow, this looks hard," she said in an amused voice, announcing her presence.

The big-green-pack guy swung around in surprise. His brown curly hair cut short on his head, his eyes wide like a deer's. No longer held back by the stick, the zombie wasted no time. Its feet left the ground as it lunged for the curly hair. The full weight of the zombie hit the guy's pack, and he fell forward with a panicked yell. Audra rolled her eyes and sidestepped the disaster. Her boot met the zombie's ribcage to roll him off the pack. The pack was bloodied by the holes the tagger had poked into the zom's body, but otherwise had protected its human underneath.

The human stumbled forward and away. His wide eyes darted between her and the zombie who was struggling to get up from its back like a turtle. Audra remained unimpressed. She ate more berries from her hand.

"Well," she said, "tie him up."

The tagger, still in an attack posture, had fear in his eyes. He looked like he might run away. His eyes searched for an escape into the forest.

"It's your zom. Tag him," she said again to encourage.

He gave her one more look, trying to read her, then straightened his posture and removed his pack. He was much taller than Audra, but his demeanor yielded to hers. He pulled out duct tape, an expensive supply, and tore off a big strip. He slunk around Audra toward the zombie's head. He attempted to cover the zombie's mouth but did not find the subject cooperative. It opened its mouth so that the tape was not wide enough. It rolled left and right. He managed to get the top lip, but the jaw opened and closed on the edge of the tape. At least the top teeth were covered. He took another piece of tape and did the same to the bottom. Feeling more comfortable, he pushed the jaw closed and employed more tape, but almost got his eyes clawed out. Maybe he forgot it had arms? Another piece of tape tied up the wrists. It was a tedious affair, and Audra watched with both amusement and impatience. Pack guy sat down next to the zombie and took a break, trying to slow his heart rate and catch his breath. Audra considered leaving once more out of boredom.

He finally rolled to his hands and knees to search the ground for the biometric reader lost in the frenzy. He sighed in relief when he found it in one piece.

This guy was a dummy.

The reader let out a long, low-tone "boop". Audra already knew what it meant.

Name: Andrew Smith
Gender: Male
DOB: 12/1/2056
Status: No inquiries

"Damn," he said, collapsing back onto the ground, too tired to stand.

"Did you expect to get something for *him*?" she asked, still trying to figure this guy out.

"What do you mean?"

"Dude, I don't mean to help my competition… but look at this guy! He's wearing farmer clothes - his family was poor before the outbreak. They are still poor. He looks like he was ugly, before, ya know, he got uglier. No one is missing this guy. You picked a bad one and wasted your time."

Pack guy looked at his ugly, poor zombie covered in tape, and sighed.

"Damn," he said again.

CHAPTER TWO

"All you have to do is scrape *this part* along the skin…" she recalled from her orientation. The short lecture and demonstration on the reader; the note to secure their hands and mouth with no explanation of how; none of it seemed like training as she stood horrified, staring down a quick and nimble zom in the overgrown field. The little girl lurched forward, almost trying to get Audra to pick a direction like she enjoyed the chase. Audra responded with a high-pitched yip and a backward jump. She tripped. With the girl at her heels, she pulled herself up with a flurry of feet and curse words.

Audra had been running from zombies for a long time now, but she had never teased one with a reader before. She stole a glance behind. The girl, just six or seven years old, was running like a crazed, murderous maniac. She was hungry, and she was not about to let her prey escape. Audra dashed into the woods hoping to navigate branches and roots more efficiently than her chaser. The girl tore through without a care, earning deep gashes on her face and arms. A thick branch lodged in her chest did nothing to stop her.

Their speeds were matched, but not their stamina. Audra's lungs ached and her left calf twinged with every undetermined number of steps. With adrenaline flowing, she realized her previous survival successes had been contingent upon not purposefully inciting trouble. She caught sight of a clearing. She forced a deep inhale and went for it. Maybe she could sprint away and gain some distance.

She got ten feet into the field before she realized her mistake.

Twenty zombies sprinkled the forty yards of field. Twenty. It must have been a camp that got overrun. Audra veered left, but it was too late. Ten had seen her, and the rest would follow their lead. Several cut her off, and the girl was on her ankles. Panic set in. She kept away from zombies for this damn reason. Who the hell did she think she was to chase zoms? This was how she died, she was sure of it. She ran toward a pine. And while it was a bad idea, it was the only idea she had. She shimmied up the tree, gaining vertical distance from her zoms. She climbed high and caught her breath as she assessed her situation.

There were no low branches for the zombies to pull on. She was twenty feet off the ground with twenty surrounding the tree. Her pack? She'd left it in the first field. To be more agile against the girl, she thought. Now she was stuck up a tree with no pack, no help, and no hope, just a dagger and a useless biometric reader. Audra resisted the urge to throw the reader into the field. It was more trouble than what it was worth. Instead, she sucked in all the air she could, then sipped in some more. She turned her face to the blue sky and let out an angry outburst against the tall pine branches above her, against a fate that had brought her here - alive up to this point, for no reason at all. The noise only sent the birds in the tree flying off and made the zombies below her spike in energy.

* * *

"You were trying to poach my zom yesterday, dude," she said with a head tilt, trying to read him.

He felt like fresh blood, new to the tagging game. But, he might also be a good actor, trying to get Audra to let her guard down. The zombie he had damaged did not appear valuable, and his pack had kept him protected when he turned. This guy could be playing her.

Instead of answering, he continued to look ruefully at his prize.

"You think if I can take the tape off, I can use some of it again?" he asked half to himself.

Audra let a smirk escape. He was good, but she would not let him change the subject.

"Yesterday?" she asked, confronting him again.

"Poach? I don't even know what that is. I thought you were in trouble. I didn't realize there were…" he hesitated, "girls… out here, tagging and stuff. I thought…" he trailed off.

"Poaching is taking someone's zombie they've targeted, stalked, and positioned. It's a jerk move. So the question is, are you a jerk?"

"No, I'm Wilfred," he said.

"I'm *not* calling you that," Audra said. "It's the damn apocalypse. No one remembers your name, you can pick a new one. And yes, there are *girls* out here," choosing his diminutive term. "We don't have enough people to be picky about genitalia."

"Ok, I'm Dwyn?" he asked.

Audra responded with a furrowed brow and a confused look.

A guy that would flip and change his name was someone worth suspicion.

He continued, "You seem to know what you're doing… will you teach me?"

He then reached for something in his pack on the ground. Audra's hand covered the handle of her knife. He resurfaced with a grain bar purchasable in the village. When he looked up, he was surprised that he had put her on the defensive. He offered her the bar. Audra let it fall to the ground but took her hand off the blade. Audra still had trouble believing he was dangerous. He scrambled for it with unnecessary motion like a teenager still growing into his limbs. He stuck it back out to her again with a smile on his face. His clean and straight teeth revealed a history of safe shelter for most of the outbreak.

Still refusing to acknowledge the food, she countered, "Who are you out here trying to find?"

"I'm just out here to help."

It was as rehearsed and as awful as his Wilfred name. If he did not want to tell her that was fine. So far, he seemed too optimistic and idealistic to be out here. Everyone had their secrets. Dwyn could have his for now. Whatever his end game, Audra figured she could handle him. A short partnership to carry out more complicated tags might just be what her ledger at Lysent needed. Afterward, she could ditch him and be that much closer.

"I get all your zombies during training," she said, seeing how he would react.

"Deal."

"You tag along, help when I need you, and then leave when you've had enough," she spouted.

"Deal," he said with increased energy.

"Touch me or my stuff and I kill you."

Her eyes narrowed and her face turned sharp with dark shadows that the sun could not erase.

"Yeah, no problem. Want a grain bar?"

Audra rolled her eyes as she turned back to camp. Randy needed to be checked.

"What about Andrew here?"

"You tag him," she called out over her shoulder.

"Will you show me how?"

What had she gotten herself into? She mustered the patience she imagined she would need for weeks to come, spun on her heel, and returned to Dwyn. After they tagged his zombie with a fresh number, she showed him how to type it into his reader. They untied his feet and did their best to remove the tape from his face without removing flesh.

"Maybe duct tape isn't the best way to go…" he concluded as he crumpled the wasted tape and flesh into a ball.

Turns out there was a lot Dwyn didn't know, including reliable ways to build a fire. Audra taught him the basics. She had nothing else to do. He was excited to be sitting next to a warm fire that evening, which kept away the bugs that plagued them most hours. They would wait on Randy's negotiations and tag more zoms in the morning. For now, it was quiet and the night undisturbed.

Audra wouldn't admit out loud that it was nice to have company for a change, but the evening was pleasant as they lounged luxuriously against a log by the fire. Audra looked up at the sky. Satellite 867, as she called it, was flying by. She and Belinda often had dreamed of escaping off this earth to what remained in the sky.

"Audra?"

She came back from space, her eyes dropping to the fire.

"Yeah, dude?"

"How cool would it be to have marshmallows?"

* * *

"We have reached a pivotal point in our lives, in our history, in our evolution."

The train had brought people in from the nearby towns to hear the important announcement. It was rumored that Lysent had figured out something monumental, maybe even how to fix the electric generators which had been down since the initial outbreak. They were doing well in the towns, keeping clean water and clean people with hard, daily work. A way to store power to run water purifiers and keep the lights on would mean a leap in their redevelopment.

While Lysent promised to improve community infrastructure for all, they still found the time to clean the front of their tall, white building and to replace the extravagantly sized glass windows in the front. Sandwiched between two uniformed guards, a small, regal woman spoke to the crowd from behind her podium. Her gray hair slicked back into a bun. Her eyes sharp.

"We confirmed this advancement several months ago, but much thought was needed to implement it in the world in which we live. While we hope this will not always be the case, it is the only way to use this advancement AND maintain our current level of living. No one wants to struggle like we have before…

"We have a cure."

The crowd broke out in incredible noise. The pause written

into the speech was much extended as people shared skepticism, celebration, even screams of terror. Some cried for their dead loved ones who would never be cured. They shouted questions to the speaker, disregarding the probability that if they were quiet, they would learn more information from the rest of the speech.

The lady was Larange Greenly. She had taken over, or perhaps had always been in charge of Lysent - at least this region. She was the one who had announced that the train system was now functional and would run its route to deliver mail and goods to the townships. She was the one who had announced that the rations for the townships had increased, decreased, then increased again. Greenly raised a hand and lowered it to signal she wanted to continue, then waited. The two hundred people quieted.

"All the townships have been sent letters to this same effect. We already know the infected are not dead. We know this because we have seen that the infected can die - sometimes of natural causes. They are sick with a virus that can be eradicated from the body. Once given a series of injections we've developed, the body returns to its normal oxygenation levels and higher brain function comes out of dormancy. The body regenerates only to the degree that the human ever could. Missing limbs will not grow back. Skin grafts may be possible in select cases.

"At this point, I would like to note, we will not be able to wake up everybody immediately.

"We barely have enough resources in the town as it is. We cannot have the entire population at our doorstep demanding food, water, and shelter. Many of those people out there are not your family. You do not know them."

Even before the speech's end, the crowd polarized in sounds of dissent and praise. Some were unhappy with the rations and space available now. They did not want others. A few were already encouraging an obligation that everyone should be awakened whatever their connection or lack thereof.

It was clear where Lysent stood.

"They do not know any better remaining how they are. And, to that effect, I'd like to explain the policy that has been put in place, balancing bringing back our loved ones into our lives, and not toppling us into famine and despair.

"You will be able to list the loved ones you are searching for who you would like cured and placed into your household. I would like to stress this first point. The people you list, if found, will be in your household and you will be financially responsible for them. You will have to care for them as they heal and transition into our new world. They will live with you. Do not wake up all the people in your old suburb. Wake up your daughter. Wake up your partner.

"Secondly, once the person is found, we will wake them up for a negotiated fee. This will demonstrate that you have the means to care for your loved ones. You will not create burdens on our society. Instead, you will help your returned ones grow in health, wealth, and contribution. This will effectively limit how many people you can wake up. Also to note, this fee does not include any medical bills for skin grafts, rehabilitation, or hospitalization.

"We are currently not taking any collaterals or payment plans. Our first phase will be cash only. After the first phase, we will match our new consensus data with projected crops. We will analyze the population data and determine if more can be cured. We will then consider other payment options.

"The only payment option that will be in effect besides cash will be a work-for-awaken plan in which a dedicated worker may be able to earn enough cash to awaken their loved one. This worker would be out in the field, finding others' loved ones who are incapable of finding them themselves. It would be dangerous work, but generously rewarded by having a loved one awakened when otherwise it would be financially infeasible."

Audra refused to live within the fences of the town, instead just entering to trade. But today she clung onto the fence, just within listening range. This was her answer and her mind reeled with the possibilities.

* * *

Dwyn, who seemed thankful that he was not "Wilfred," learned quickly. Audra first helped him whittle down his pack weight since he couldn't run any decent speed with it on. She removed over half of his belongings much to Dwyn's balking. She put it in another bag and hid it in the brush.

"We can come back in two weeks and you can get anything you want from it," she encouraged.

After two weeks he didn't even want to go look inside the bag. Audra was right.

And while she thought she would use him as bait for a couple two-person zombies and then send him on his way, he was showing promise as a partner. She taught him the basic strategies: Bait & Switch, Loop-de-loop, and Space Jam. They then moved onto more advanced two-person strategies like Leap Frog. Despite tagging nearly a dozen zombies, they didn't find anyone of worth.

They had been out there for three weeks, waiting on Randy's negotiations, but they finally had an answer. Audra considered the length of negotiation with a grim smile. Maybe the family did not have enough money. They were scrambling for more and trying to negotiate a lower price. But another likely scenario was that the family was rich and yes, they wanted to wake up Randy and a few other relatives, but they were not expecting to pay *that* much for Randy. It was amazing how many people did things out of obligation to someone that only knows "eat humans" on a daily basis. That would come out in the negotiation when they needed to put a price on their "loved" one. Most of the negotiation was the personal journey of the healthy person. A bunch of bullshit.

Audra made up the time lost in negotiations with her delivery speed. While others took multiple days to get in and out of the town, Audra was fast even with a zombie in tow. In her childhood school, she hadn't been a runner. It was a skill she learned and loved out here. Audra had met many people who hated running. It meant fear. It meant running for their lives. And Audra sort of got that, but she also knew she had always survived. She had always outrun her troubles. And that was something in her pocket. The people who did not want to run anymore stayed in their townships, got rations delivered by a fence-protected train, and negotiated with their loved ones' lives.

The trio ran along the ten-foot-high fence towards the main township. There were several townships now, all along the trade route. Following the track was the most direct and cleared path. It was also a great place to catch up on gossip from the other taggers as they came in and out of towns. Randy followed along behind them, occasionally getting caught along the chain links that tore at his clothes. It was a wonder he was in such good condition. Besides taggers, an occasional lone hiker returned from a resupply. Some people did not transition well from surviving in the wilderness back into the strict towns with measured rations and daily reports. Audra felt the same.

Even ten feet away on the opposite side of the fence, she felt the buzz of the electric track. Audra questioned if it actually made noise, but at the least, it vibrated and made her hair stand on end. She slowed to look back at the train. Randy tried to take a bite from her neck. She shook her head and returned to speed. The fifteen cars of a sleek silver train passed. It carried each week's rations, mail (subject to Lysent perusal), and trade goods. At times people used it to get from town to town, but it was an expensive endeavor for the sentimental. The train and its technology galvanized Lysent as the organization in charge after people began rebuilding.

No one could remember if Lysent had always owned the trains, but they owned a lot explicitly or under an umbrella in the world before. The train hadn't broken down with the rest of the modern world. Solar energy collected by the rails and train cars supplemented the electromagnetic rail system. It was self-sustained. They only needed two fences to keep zombies from piling up on the tracks, and a periodic patrol to clear it. At first, that meant killing the zombies. But now that everyone was aware the zombies were not dead, and instead, alive and recoverable, more humane ways were required to keep the zombies from being an inconvenience to the fastest trade route. Lysent built corrals out of sight to confine the zoms in the name of safety. Everyone was thankful for Lysent's reach and capabilities.

Audra understood that they would not have progressed at such a rapid rate without them, before or after the outbreak, but that did not mean they were worth the price of their autonomy and agency. They were too organized and too meddling. They left an awful taste in her mouth. But, here she was, working for them, like any government worker, just one who did not bathe often, and ran around chasing and running from zombies most of the day. Audra would drop off Randy, receive payment, and leave as quickly as possible. Their partnership was a necessity, but not one she needed to prolong.

Not even a couple miles in, a raunchy looking guy, thin and haggard, walked toward them from the opposite direction. He complimented their nice find, Randy's business suit dirty and flapping open.

"Watch out for Audra, though," he said toward Dwyn, "She'll leave you out to dry."

Dwyn made no comment but noticed Audra give Randy a little yank to increase his pace.

After an hour or so, Dwyn was forced to walk. He was not a conditioned runner like Audra. She kept going. It was part of the deal. He could tag along as long as he wanted and had the ability to do so. He knew where she was heading. Audra finished the thirty miles and camped not too far from the tracks. A couple hours later, after it was dark, he caught up with her. She had already eaten, her food tied up in the tree, and she was sleeping, hugging her pack in her tent.

Audra was up at dawn. She checked the cloudless sky and muddied her face and arms to protect her from the sun. She gave Dwyn a little kick, knowing he had come in late. He groaned but did not move.

"I'm heading out. I'll see you at the township."

"Mreh."

CHAPTER THREE

Hands bound with neat twine and mouth covered with a red handkerchief, Belinda followed her sister obediently into the Lysent plaza. Audra had wiped the protective mud off their skin and combed their hair. The human bite on Belinda's right forearm had been cleaned and dressed. They both needed to look their best for the committee. But, no amount of preening could disguise Belinda's eyes - frozen wide, lifeless, and gray.

Against the plaza, behind a waist-high barrier, several people shouted angry words at them.

"Don't wake her up! It's against God's will!"

Audra knew there would be dissenters opposed to curing. They believed the infected had proven themselves incapable of surviving in this world. Reviving them would be a waste of resources. Audra walked past them without a word. She did not completely disagree with them.

The protesters were not allowed in the plaza and as the sisters approached the entrance to the main white building, the yelling faded. A sign posted on the door stated, "NO

INFECTED THIS WAY".

Audra glanced around and found no one to help. She was sure she shouldn't leave her sister unsupervised outside. Lysent would not approve and she didn't trust the protesters just outside the barriers. Before she made a decision, a tall thin man in uniform robes met them at the bottom of the white porch. The man raised his eyebrows at the pair. Audra had thought she had cleaned them both up, but they remained a stark contrast to his crisp, clean glow. He waved them to the side of the building and Audra followed, no longer eager to step inside.

Beside the building stood a small metal outhouse. It was the perfect size for one person. Audra held back and Belinda bumped into her. Would they be separated? The thin man noticed the hesitation in her steps. He raised his bushy eyebrows once more, but his voice was friendly and assuring.

"What's her name?"

"Belinda."

"That's a lovely name. Belinda will be really grateful that you took such good care of her while she was sick. She looks great. It must have been hard to keep her in such good condition."

Audra gave a grateful smile. It had been hard to keep Belinda out of trouble. She was always wandering off toward any noise or movement in her peripheral. At first, Audra had kept her in her tent at night, but Belinda never tired. She was constantly shuffling. Eventually, she'd convinced herself that Belinda would be all right tied up outside the tent with a tarp draped loosely around her to keep off the rain. It was Audra's least favorite part of corralling Belinda, but Belinda didn't seem to care.

"Belinda will be safe inside while you meet with the Awakening Committee," he said as he opened the shed door.

Audra weighed her options. She had promised her mother she would keep Belinda safe. This could be the only way to revive her, but it could also be a trap. The thin man tested the ties as Belinda shuffled in, and an image of an alive, kicking, and screaming Belinda protesting her confinement forced its way into Audra's mind as the door clicked shut.

Audra felt small and childlike following the tall man back to the main entrance. She was not sure if she was supposed to be this small, or if she hadn't gotten enough nutrition during her puberty and adolescence. Belinda was still much taller than her, despite her slowed metabolism in the last year.

The yells kicked up again as they turned the corner.

"Keep them dead!"

Audra expected her escort to dismiss the protests conversationally, given her purpose and his business, but he did not. He only motioned her inside when they reached the door. The front lobby had a tall ceiling and matching windows to let the light in. It was a nice feature. Given that electricity was rationed, the sun was preferable. Audra felt more and more inadequate as her muddy feet left marks on the white marble and she saw the clean and bright lady behind the desk. Would they give her the time of day?

"Hi Clyde, someone looking for their parents?" the lady behind the front desk asked.

Her dark curly hair bounced as her fingers flitted from one stack of paper to the next on her desk. Audra was reminded of the doctor's office of her childhood, or the few times she had visited her mom at work. She hadn't realized people still had office jobs.

"No, she brought her own. Would like to see the committee, I imagine."

He looked at Audra, who nodded approvingly.

"OK, well, answer this questionnaire, sweetie, and we'll get you in as soon as possible."

She guided Audra to one of the chairs. As she handed her a clipboard and pen, she whispered into her ear.

"Do you know how to read and write, sweetie?"

"Yes ma'am," Audra said automatically.

That was the truth, but she had not done so in the last three years. Her eyes were trained to follow movement and as she looked at the paper, the letters swam around. She took a deep breath and willed the first word to stop moving. After a few slow, stumbling sentences, she improved.

The questionnaire was blunt and clinical. It asked her name, age, previous occupation, and current living arrangements. It asked her how long she had known the infected, and what she intended to do with the infected once awakened. The final questions stung.

"Do you have at least 1 million credits to awaken the infected person?" No.

"If yes, will the transaction be cash or through the bank?"

"If no, are you willing to discuss a payment plan?" Yes.

Audra returned the paperwork. Initially impressed by her literacy, the receptionist glanced at the bottom of the form to confirm her suspicion. Audra had no money.

"You can wait back at your seat. The committee will review your application and meet with you in the next hour or so. They have lunch right now."

Wait? What people had the luxury of waiting anymore? She thought of her low food rations. She thought of checking on her sister. Perhaps she could come back later? She decided not to be a difficult person. She waited.

Eventually, the lady at the front desk escorted her down the hall. She roughly whispered quick advice to her as if she had just decided to help.

"There's a big group but you only have to convince the one."

Before Audra could ask which one, the receptionist swung open a pair of doors. There sat seven men and women in robes behind a long desk. A single chair faced them. Audra sat and nodded. A soft jab in her shoulder told her she should stand back up. After a few awkward moments, the lady in the center gave a small smile and told their rude guest she could be seated. Audra recognized her gray slicked back hair and small dark eyes. It was Larange Greenly, the woman who made all decisions impacting the towns and delivered the news - good or bad - on the plaza front.

"The infected is your sister?" she asked, her voice's pitch rising in amusement.

Audra opened her mouth to answer, but Greenly did not wait.

"Why do you want to awaken her?"

"She is my sister and I love her."

Her response was met with snickers and patronizing looks. Audra swallowed her anger. She needed them to be on her side.

A man to Greenly's left with a full white beard cleared his throat.

"We understand you do not have the full payment yet. How much do you have?"

He sat back ready to do calculations in his head.

"Well, sir, I have no credits to my name."

He sat back up and leaned toward her.

"Then why are you wasting our time?"

It was easy for them to sit in these meetings, making

assessments and dictating people's lives behind their table and walls. They did not understand what lay beyond the fences. Their undeserved power could not be overturned, though. Audra realized she was losing their patience and possibly her chance.

"I'm not wasting your time. I'm a good runner, sir. I can run a 7-minute mile in the woods. I can run twenty-five miles one day, and thirty the next. I've been out there for three years. I would be a good tagger.

"Let me tag zombies for you in exchange for waking up my sister."

Audra looked at each committee person. Most seemed unconvinced, but Greenly's mild amusement had grown into a sly smile.

"Let's hope your abilities match the grit we see here," she said, not missing Audra's simmering attitude.

"An ambitious girl. She may be one to watch. Give her a contract. Committee dismissed," announced Greenly.

"Wait, that's it?" she asked as the receptionist ushered her to the lobby.

"Yes, I'll give you the contract to look over. It says as a tagger, you get ten percent of the negotiated price of an awakened zombie. You can get that money in cash or put it toward awakening your sister. Your sister stays here and you pay rent each month, pulled from your account. If more than two months pass without communication, Lysent reserves the right to put down your sister."

"How many people do I need to catch and bring in to awaken my sister?"

"If you brought them all in tomorrow and everyone, including your sister, went for the average price, ten people would do. Unfortunately, rent and indenture fees add up quickly."

"Rent and indenture fees? Aren't those the same thing?"

"No, unfortunately, they are not."

"So, practically, how many people will I need?"

"If you're good at it, maybe fifty?"

"What if I keep Belinda somewhere else and don't pay rent?"

"It is part of the deal. She is collateral for the biometric reader we are lending you. We guarantee she stays in her current condition, barring death. If she stays somewhere else, she may degrade. You will be out running and won't be able to care for her. Did you have a secondary place in mind?"

"No."

Audra considered how much care her sister required, especially the hunting. Belinda couldn't eat anything farmed or gathered. She looked over the contract. Even with a lack of formal education, she surmised it was not in her favor. It was a piling of debt she might never repay.

She thought of her sister, outside in the dark closet. It had seemed a fool's errand to keep her body for so long. She sat and shed a tear for every time she considered ending her sister's existence. Would it have been for her own selfish desires? Did she really think a person needed to pass on from this world to be complete? Audra had her answer, a promise to her mother and promise of a cure. Settling in a town, Belinda would thrive behind walls, under roofs, and behind fences. They would learn occupations. Belinda would be a seamstress. Audra would do labor and mail runs for extra money. It would be the life that Belinda deserved.

She signed the paper.

* * *

Audra realized the committee agreed to make her a tagger because there was nothing to lose on their end. Someone would bring in her biometric reader for a small reward fee when she died trying to tag her first zom. And then, they would destroy Belinda. But she proved them wrong with every tag and return.

Audra tugged Randy. Her quads twinged with each footfall and her back ached, but she could handle more speed for a few more moments. Even if Dwyn had not slept in, he would not have been able to keep up with her. Randy matched her speed without complaint. She would be rid of him soon and tomorrow he would wake up under the watchful eyes of scientists.

The dissenters outside the plaza had changed their chants in the last two years.

"Don't add to the rich!"

"Lysent owns us!"

With every awakening, another was added to the corporation's community who required food, energy, and clothes. They argued that their job never matched their burden on the community. No one ever woke up and became a farmer. They were part of the elite, part of the rich. Audra did not disagree with them, but she rolled her eyes at them all the same. These protesters who yelled at her went home just a few hundred feet away from Lysent, cozy within their fences. They hassled her as if she had a choice.

It was old routine now. Audra ran Randy over to the metal closet without an escort. It was unoccupied. She secured him and sauntered into the lobby. She greeted Rosie who was sitting at the desk, shuffling through paperwork strewn all over.

"I've brought Randy… I mean, Randolph… Ludington?"

"Ludington, Ludington… Audra…" Rosie said as she shuffled through yet another set of papers and folders behind her. She found a blue folder and pulled it out and placed it on top of all the other papers on her desk, the easy cause of her clutter. She gave some of the papers in the folder to Audra.

"Audra! You got me another winner?!" called out Clyde as he entered the lobby. Audra just smiled politely and started her paperwork without banter. Clyde and Rosie exchanged knowing glances. Audra would withdraw against her Finder's Fee today.

Clyde returned from his review, assessment in hand. He compared his notes with Audra's form. Their rating on body condition differed.

"That bite is bad, Audra."

The sullen expression on Audra's face erupted into an amiable grin. Her laughter reflected their years of friendship.

"C'mon man! He has been out there for *years*, and he looks amazing. That bite is not my fault. That's how he… y'know got infected."

"He does look great, besides the bite," Clyde said with pride in his voice as if he had anything to do with it.

"You'll graft it, it'll make a good scar for his story. The men like that, right?"

"Yeah, I guess so. I'll knock mine back a grade."

"Thanks, Clyde. I owe you one."

"You bring in the best bodies, Audra. You're great out there."

"I hope I don't have to be out there much longer."

"Speaking of, do you want your payment, minus rent, in Belinda's deposit? It's a nice one."

"No, I'll take half with me."

"Well, progress is progress, I guess, Audra," he half scolded her.

Audra did not reply, but her face fell and she lost her twinkle.

They finished the transaction and Audra tucked the several credits in a pouch near her breast. Clyde was already outside prepping Randy for his inspection by the Awakening Committee. Audra turned before she walked out the door.

"Oh, if a guy comes in here looking for me in say… two hours?"

"I'll let him know where to find you," said Rosie with a pained face.

"Thanks," she said, refusing to acknowledge Rosie's concern.

* * *

Still in the tree she'd scrambled up to escape the herd, Audra concluded that days would pass before there would be a passerby. And chances were a passerby would avoid her group of twenty-one zombies at all costs. The surrounding trees were not large enough or close enough for her to reach. So there she sat, perched on the first weight-bearing branch, midway up the tree. She would have to get out of this herself. And the only way was down, now, before she became dehydrated and exhausted.

Audra tied up her hair and with a deep breath, she pulled out her dagger. When her family had abandoned the car and walked into the forest, her mother had given her a dagger for safety. Now, Audra always had at least two, one to use and one to lose. Belinda used hers to whittle small figurines.

Audra positioned herself upside down, her legs wrapped around the rough bark of the tree. Looking straight down she did not see people, at least not salvageable people, just death in multitude, enthusiastic about her approach.

The clearance between the crown of her head and her zombie friends was minimal once she got close enough to leverage her weapon. The sun had not been kind to those in the field. The first corpse, weathered and shredded, reached its lanky upper limbs toward her. Audra held fast to the dagger and stabbed squarely in the crown of the head and yanked back. It became inanimate but did not fall down. Other bodies braced against it and began to climb. Audra repositioned and looked to the zombie closest to her weapon. Possibly a woman. Her dry teeth made a clicking noise which Audra ended. She crossed the dagger across her body and moved it into a third.

With those dead, Audra retreated up the tree to gain a little space and rest. The inverted warrior looked upon the battlefield. The trio had now fallen. Others stood on them, gaining a few inches of height. Audra shuffled back down. She was determined to get five more before she climbed back up to a branch to let the blood rush back to her legs and away from her head.

She pierced another and received a face full of blood. Her supporting hand reached in a panic. She slipped inches downward before her legs caught her fall. Squinting her eyes and pursing her lips, she willed it not to go up her nose. Her stomach turned and her mouth gaped as she gagged. But it did not matter in the next moments as another lunged. She swung shallowly toward the nasal cavity, slowing it down and getting her dagger stuck.

She yanked back hard and popped herself in the face with the handle when it released. The blood from her nose mingled with the blood from her kill and tickled all her senses and those of her friends. She took a moment to wipe the blood off her face and into her hair. The bugs were already collecting around her, attracted to the smell. Dreaded gnats flying into the fluids and into her eyes. Despite the hole in his face, her pursuer still needed a final blow.

The stupidity and heaviness of what she was undertaking sank in. Tears washed her eyes clean. Audra took a deep, gasping breath and reached for her injured target, splattered with bloodstained tears.

* * *

The burly man on the other side of the bar nodded to the door. Audra did not have to move from her draped position over the bar's surface to know Dwyn had arrived. He approached her peripheral, cautious in this new environment. The barkeep pointed to the vat of foul smelling moonshine behind him.

"Looks like she has had enough for both of us," Dwyn declined.

Audra rolled her eyes in his full view.

"Did you turn in Randy?" he asked.

"Mm-hm."

"Did you get the money?"

"Mh-hm."

"Did you give it all to this guy?"

Audra peeled her face off the wood to glare and curse. Her intensity smelled of anger and moonshine.

Dwyn tipped his chin at the bartender and walked out.

CHAPTER FOUR

Audra tried to find the sun through the trees and clouds. She judged she had about an hour of daylight left to pull Debbie Lancer. She ignored the temptation to set up camp early. While most of Audra's life was already well-practiced in camping, staying out of sight, and finding food and water, escorting a zombie to Lysent was still new to her skill set. She tugged on her leashed zom. A sack on Debbie's head gave a small amount of protection to Audra's backside, but it blocked Debbie's sight, and that led to many falls, sometimes atop Audra. Audra settled for a longer lead and constantly checked the distance between her and the unsecured face of Debbie.

With a few tags to her name, Audra noticed the underlying theme. The families were rich and the zoms were gorgeous. Even in death and weathered exposure, Debbie had kept her figure, face symmetry, and thick hair. The rich and pretty ruled this new world, too.

Audra managed to not get eaten for one more hour as they trudged closer to the corporation for her payout. With a sigh,

Audra settled in front of her perfectly crafted fire. At least she could do that well. She planned to move only if the smoke drifted her way for too long. She let darkness engulf her. With a few moments of peace and no immediate problems, the thoughts flooded in.

It was her fault.

No, she never should have been put in that situation.

Still, it was her fault.

The thoughts churned and Audra's eyes welled. She stared deep into the fire but it did not register. All she saw was red. A wall of red and it warmed her head until she felt she was on fire. And then the air escaped her. An inhale did not follow. How could she sit here while her sister rotted within herself? She would give anything to make the pain leave, to have her sister here and well. Heaviness and impossibility sank in.

A large, triumphant growl filled her ear. She snapped around to find Debbie inches from her face. Audra pushed her away and assessed the bodily damage. Debbie had been bound at the edge of the campsite. She had pulled her wrists loose of her ropes and the majority of her flesh in the process. Skin and muscle flapped around as she pulled herself to Audra. No one would be able to sew her up and Lysent would not wake a double hand amputee. Someone had loved Debbie and Audra had destroyed her. It was her fault. Audra yelled out and in an instant had pulled out her knife from her boot and launched herself at the crawling remains.

The two wrestled on the ground for a few moments. With each glancing blow from the floppy hands or attack from the jaws, Audra got a renewed sense of strength, a strength drained by this world. Then she stabbed her.

Again. And again.

Until Debbie was no longer Debbie.

Audra saw a different shade of red, but her thoughts were quieted in the blood and stench. She passed out next to the corpse before the cyclic thoughts roared again.

* * *

Audra emerged a few days later from the hole. She took inventory of her pack. She had no money. She rummaged to find her cooking pot, hickory nuts, and a couple of worn photographs of her family from when the world was normal. It could have been worse. Sometimes it was worse. Audra would need to take a job to get a few more supplies before she returned to the wilderness to tag. She stepped out of the town, past the fences to keep out the dead, and found a familiar creek. She rinsed her face, switched out to a clean shirt, and headed back into the market. There she would find the jobs she needed.

As she searched for the unofficial post, a voice called out behind her.

"Do you always fall out like that?" Dwyn asked casually.

"Not always," she said shortly, trying to hide her shame behind impatience.

She did not have to prove anything to Dwyn. The world had gone to shit. She could too, occasionally. It didn't seem to stop him from following her.

Once she remembered which town she was in, she found the unofficial post. The fastest way to mail a letter from town to town was the train. But the train only ran once a week and all mail was subject to review. Lysent didn't allow correspondence that disrespected the company or promoted outside governments or groups. They explained that this was their right because they had invested so much in rebuilding. If you wanted to create another system of government, go somewhere else and create your own infrastructure.

If you wanted to send a letter during the week or under the nose of the governing body, you needed to send it with a traveler. A tagger's ability and constant need for a quick buck made them excellent unofficial mail-keeps. Audra had earned a reputation for being one of the fastest mail servicers when she was available. Without a body in tow, Audra promised same-day delivery.

They entered the house to find a gruff looking man. His wide grin competed with his large frizzy beard in magnitude.

"I heard you were in town," he said motioning to Audra. His smile wavered as he looked to Dwyn with suspicion.

"He's with me," she answered his unasked question. "You got any mail for me?"

"Of course, I started gathering it this morning. Told them it'd be a few hours before you'd be ready," he said hunting for the hidden folder of mail. He found it and she tucked it into her bag.

"Money on receipt," he said as he disappeared into the back room.

Audra rolled her eyes and headed out.

"I just need to grab my pack," said Dwyn as he ran around the corner.

Audra considered running off without him but decided against it. She needed to eat. Under the shade of oak trees outside the fences, she opened hickory nuts while she examined the destinations on the envelopes. There were three different townships, seven envelopes in total. She could get this done in a day, no problem. She'd buy supplies, sleep near the last town, then head out to tag another zombie in the morning. Audra tucked the envelopes back into her bag and focused on pulling the last of the nut meat from its shells as Dwyn approached with his pack in tow.

"I thought you left without me again," he said, out of breath.

"Thought about it."

Audra and Dwyn started with a steady pace toward the first township, using the train tracks as their easy guide. It was not two miles later when Audra keeled over and vomited her hickory nuts into a bush.

"I brought you extra water," Dwyn offered.

Audra took it in silence. She drank the whole bottle and sat there for ten minutes. Ten minutes was another mile they could have covered. Dwyn offered to help steady her as she stood, but she refused. She ran another half mile and vomited off to the side. She did not stop this time but kept running.

For once, Dwyn could keep up.

The sun had set well before Audra and Dwyn made it to the last township. Audra held out her left hand and ran it along the chain link fence to keep the correct trajectory. Dwyn ran staggered to her right, keeping an ear out for zombies. They heard them in the distance, mildly interested in the light "chink, chink" the fence made against Audra's hand. When they neared the township, a large floodlight flashed and blinded them. A bow and arrow hid behind the light. She waved to signal their vitality. As they approached the gate, a stern eye greeted them.

"Why are you coming in so late?"

"We got held up. We're sorry. Can we stay for the night?"

He said nothing but motioned to someone below and the gate opened.

"Thanks. Do you need any water?" Audra offered.

She wanted to stay on the good side of the guards. You never knew when your ass would be in trouble and you'd need a speedy gate opening. He smiled his thanks but waved them on.

Audra and Dwyn walked into the dark center of town. It was the smallest township and everyone had already retreated to their homes. Audra found the location that served as the underground post office and gave it a small knock. Inside, she heard rustling. Dwyn looked reluctant.

"Maybe we could leave it to morning?" Dwyn mumbled.

A woman opened the door. She wore a night robe and a face twisted in confusion and annoyance.

"Mail," Audra stated.

The lady opened the door wider and removed herself from the doorway to let them pass. Inside with the door closed, Audra let one of her arms out of the pack straps and let the pack fall to her side. She pulled out the mail and handed it over. The lady received it and shuffled to a hutch to retrieve their money.

Their eyes met as she gave Audra the credits.

"I've been told to ask you to stay at your camp in the morning. There is someone who would like to speak with you."

Audra nodded but was not impressed. Lots of people wanted to use her skill set. They often couldn't pay more than what Lysent offered.

The runners left as quickly as they had arrived.

Rather than annoy the gatekeeper once more, Audra and Dwyn climbed over the fence that protected the township. They landed with a thump on the other side, tired and ready for sleep. All the running, and in Audra's case - vomiting, had taken its toll. Despite her exhaustion, she couldn't miss Dwyn's anxious fidgeting.

"What's going on?" she asked, daring him to delay her bedtime.

"I don't know if we should stick around and meet that person."

"It's probably no one. I'm not staying for them - I'm staying for sleep and for the market tomorrow."

She kicked away sticks and rocks from what would be her tent's foundation. Out of the corner of her eye, she noticed Dwyn hadn't even begun his camp setup. He shuffled from foot to foot. He was still not telling her something. Audra stopped and looked him in the eye.

"Do you know this person, Dwyn?"

He returned her look and exhaled loudly. Then the words rushed out before he changed his mind.

"Yes. I was sent by them to recruit someone for the next step in the plan."

Audra's eyebrows rose. She took one step forward and punched him in the left eye. Dwyn staggered back from the force, grabbing his eye as he doubled over.

"See," he said. "We need someone tough. We don't have anyone tough."

And then he blurted out his worry.

"But I don't know if you should meet her because you're um… not that reliable. I don't know if you're the best person."

Tiredness and sickness overwhelmed what remained of Audra's anger. Dwyn's secrets were about to unravel and she found she didn't even care. She wanted to sleep.

"I'll punch you again in the morning," she said as she threw herself into her tent.

* * *

A shadow across her tent woke Audra to the bright morning. She didn't usually sleep in, but she didn't usually sleep in vomit-soaked clothes, either. Audra pulled her spare shirt out of her pack. She would scrub the other in the creek after breakfast. Outside, Dwyn's shadow stopped moving as she lifted her arms over her head. Audra could not stifle her sly smile. He was watching her silhouette undress. Dwyn was not unattractive, and he had gotten even fitter in the weeks they trained together. She put on her shirt, but then stretched her arms up again and leaned back to show off her figure behind the safety of the canvas tent.

She took a deep breath and asked herself what she was doing. This guy was recruiting her for a harebrained scheme. She rolled her eyes. She yanked her arms down and wrestled with her pack. Dwyn suddenly began moving as well, making too much noise to be convincing.

Like she did every morning, she rolled up her things and placed them in her pack, except her t-shirt. It was nasty, possibly worth replacing in the market. It was soft and worn though, perfect for running. Maybe she could salvage it after she scraped off the hickory nut meat. She threw the shirt out of her tent with her pack. Her quads ached from dehydration as she climbed out of the tent. Drinking all of Dwyn's treated water did little to mitigate her head's throbbing, incited by the day's brightness.

She had not even finished breaking down her tent when a woman approached their camp. A shawl protected her salt and pepper hair from the sun. Her age was difficult to determine. Even at a distance, her skin and eyes were clear and young. She carried herself upright, not yet fighting the gravity of age. She gathered elderberries as she walked, her excuse for being outside the township today. Audra continued to break down her tent. Instinct demanded she be ready to retreat, to run away, even from an innocent-looking lady with a bucket of berries.

Audra finished packing and stood to confront the

newcomer. Audra was a head shorter, and she wondered once again if malnutrition or genetics had stunted her own height. The lady tipped half of her berry stock into Dwyn's empty bowl.

"I will need to come back with some," she said explaining her half-generosity.

"Thanks!" said Dwyn, thrusting his hand into the formerly empty tin bowl.

Audra ignored his trusting actions. She did not have time for him. She turned her eyes back to the woman.

"Hi, Audra. It is truly a pleasure to meet you. I'm Vesna. Dwyn sent word about you." She smiled but eyed Dwyn.

"So Dwyn's his real name, huh?"

Audra perched on a log and grabbed a handful of berries from Dwyn. She popped a couple in her mouth and dared Vesna to continue.

"Audra," Vesna repeated her name to garner rapport, "I heard you are an indentured tagger. You have a loved one infected?"

Audra stared into her eyes, not allowing her an answer or emotion. Vesna was trying to propose her idea in terms of Audra's desires. Audra knew the trick. She used that trick all the time. Vesna returned the silent stare and calculated her. She dropped her strategy and picked up another.

"I lead a small group that questions the current system of government. Lysent should not control who wakes up, or keep us from our loved ones. We want to change that."

"And how will you change that? Lysent is everything."

"Lysent works to limit resources and the population. We have a plan to cure many, all at once. It will topple the current economics on which the corporation gains their power."

Audra did not hear past "cure."

"You have antidotes?"

"We have a scientist who worked with the antidote. She is confident she can synthesize her own batch. We just need help to set up everything. We need someone to clear out this old laboratory…"

Audra's excitement faded. They did not have a cure. They had someone who talked. Vesna could tell she was losing her recruit. She once again changed tactics.

"You were young when it happened, but think about where you went when you got sick."

"The doctor?"

"Where was the doctor?"

"In the white corporation building."

"Lysent owned so many things. Medicine, technology, transportation, communication. They were tasked to fight the disease. The world was decimated and yet, they came out on top. How?"

Vesna's voice held an insinuation.

"You don't think they fought as hard as they could have?"

"More than that," Vesna answered with grimness. "They developed it."

Audra had met many conspiracy enthusiasts, but Vesna appeared to be in a category all her own.

"Lysent started the infection? Why?"

"To diminish the population and rebuild the world? I don't know. Maybe they didn't mean for it to go this far, but now they control everything. They're even reversing their work as they see fit. How else do you think they had the antidote?"

"Because they researched. You just said you had a scientist who was part of the research."

"No. There was no research. My scientist found out that

there was just a stockpile of antidotes, a formula, and workers brewing up new doses."

Vesna's eyes were fervent that her potential recruit listen and understand.

Even if all this was true, Audra was not sure she cared. She had no positive feelings toward Lysent, but was this a fight she wanted?

"Sorry, lady. I'm not interested."

She pulled her pack onto her back to go to market. Vesna made noises of disagreement.

"Please, Audra."

"I'm not going to tell anyone about your pretty little plan. Just leave me out of it."

Vesna gathered her courage as Audra turned to leave.

"You're never going to awaken your sister through indentured tagging, especially if you drink away half your findings."

Audra ignored her and kept walking. She needed supplies.

CHAPTER FIVE

The family of four created their new home. It was a large tarp on sticks, a cleared area for a fire, a line to hang clothes, and a few logs to sit on, but it was more than they'd had in months. The parents argued over their decision to leave Atlanta, but with each passerby coming from there, it became evident they had left just in time. The city had become a stronghold of zombies. The family's chance of survival increased hidden in the woods, even if their camping experience was limited to a couple of poorly executed family vacations.

Dad, Audra, and Belinda headed for the lake to fish. Belinda complained that she was tired of fish. Why couldn't their dad catch a land animal or a bird? Audra kept her mouth shut and followed the almost familiar path to the water.

Halfway there, they heard rustling up ahead and a burst of noise as birds took off from a bush. Belinda screamed, turned tail, and ran back to camp to her mother. Audra and her father did not stop her. They could catch more fish without her.

The pond was big but maybe not large enough to be called a

lake. Audra didn't know the size requirements for labeling bodies of water. They baited their hooks, both secretly wishing that Belinda had not run off with the third. The duo could have manned three. They sat in silent but comfortable camaraderie.

Audra and her father understood each other. Audra watched her father take care of his wife and his children. She modeled her care for Belinda on his - giving opportunities for growth while keeping her safe. Her dad was teaching them how to use different weapons. Her mom loved the machete for its big swing and power. Audra loved her dagger for she was quick and could anticipate the moves of her attacker. Their dad gave Belinda many weapons to try, but her constitution did not seem affected by any equipment provided.

Breaking the silence, as if they had both been discussing Belinda's difficulties without words, her dad surprised her.

"Audra-sweets, if something happens to your mom and me, which is likely given our situation… you need to know something."

Her father paused, trying to find the right words. He stared out into the pond as if the view was more thought-provoking than it was.

"Belinda… she will not make it in this world. And that will not be your fault. OK?"

Audra disagreed with her father's assessment of his older daughter, but she did not argue outright. Belinda was fearful, but Audra had been too when it all began. Belinda would come around. She just needed more time. Her family needed to support her, not give up. Belinda may not be the best fit for this new world, but that did not mean she did not deserve to be in it. The pair would make it through, together. She wished Belinda had ventured back to the pond, to prove their dad wrong, if only in this instance.

Audra knew she could help Belinda, but she nodded with obedience and respect. Then, she wished for more fish.

* * *

Dwyn caught up with her heated pace as she entered the market. Audra did not acknowledge his accompaniment as she purchased chicken jerky and oat bars for emergencies and en route convenience. She would get most of her food from the woods, where it was free.

Her interaction with Vesna reminded her why she did not want to dwell in the villages. The tenants had only been awake for an hour, but she had already grown tired of them. She detested their grumblings and protests when they did nothing to change it. Everyone had opinions but stayed safe within the confines of the fences. At least Dwyn had ventured out to find her. With her new food items tucked into the side pockets of her pack within easy reach, she ran out of the town with Dwyn at her heels.

That Dwyn had an ulterior motive did not surprise Audra. Everyone had one, including her. She'd taken in Dwyn to pull off a few two-person jobs, get tags she would not get otherwise, and though she would not admit it, have company once in a while. Since Belinda, she realized everyone had personal agendas. And now she knew Dwyn's.

"Hey, I'm sorry that I wasn't honest with you. My name is Dwyn. I was sent to find someone to help clear out a laboratory that no one uses anymore. We want to synthesize the antidote there and cure everyone we can. I don't understand why you're upset. Do you want to keep working for Lysent?"

Audra's face flushed. She did not want to keep working for

Lysent. They were awful, but there was no way around it.

"No," she spat out, "but what can any of us do?"

"Well, I can't do much," he admitted, "but, maybe you can."

She hated the village's inhabitants for their compliance, but only because she saw the same in herself. Lysent was taking advantage of everyone, including the taggers. The system was tilted against her, but it was her only concrete choice now. No one else awakened people, just the corporation. What else was she going to do besides swallow the hypocrisy of it all for her sister and hope to catch a break that would set her ahead of Lysent's rotten curve?

Audra came to a halt. Dwyn was slow to react and circled back around. She didn't know why she needed him to understand. Maybe she felt guilty.

"This is my best option right now. You're not recruiting me."

Dwyn was not ready to give up.

"OK, what if we *hire* you? Give you a payout after you clear out the laboratory? You don't have to believe in us to accept our money."

Audra's eyes squinted. If she got ahead on Belinda's rent, she could make leeway into the awakening fee.

"I'll think about it," she said. "Are you still interested in tagging?"

"Why?"

"I want to travel I-16 toward the Savannah port, but tagging is a two-person deal there. Do you want to come, or are you, uh, done with whatever it is you're doing with me?"

Dwyn smiled, "Well, I've never been to Savannah."

Audra started her run again. Dwyn pulled up alongside her, instead of chasing. Audra was excited to pick through the many cars sitting on I-16. There would be easy tags along the evacuation route. Maybe they had families who'd survived.

There was one thing that kept bothering her.

"Are you actually bad at tagging and running or was that a ruse?"

"Wait, I'm not *that* bad, am I?"

Audra scoffed and kicked up her heels a little higher.

* * *

Today was the day. Audra packed their supplies in happy silence as Belinda, on this rare occasion, cooked breakfast over a fire she had crafted herself. It caught just enough to warm yesterday's leftovers with water poured over, but Audra was happy for the break. Audra was always the one gathering the wood, building the fires, and cooking the meals. Belinda stopped muttering to herself and looked up from her fussing to smile at Audra. Audra smiled back.

Yesterday while collecting firewood, Audra had discovered a zombie couple and their campground. There was no perpetrator in sight. One must have gotten bit and was too scared to tell the other. Or perhaps, they went down together. Whatever it was, the sisters didn't know or care. What they did care about was their available supplies, particularly their tent. A real tent! Not a patched tarp propped up by sticks, but a real, modern tent.

Neither dared to say it was their last night under the tarp as they finished the rabbit and frog stew. More substantial than berries and leaves, it would stick to their bones for the day. Ready to tackle the Zombie Couple, the two threw on their packs. Belinda did not even complain about its weight compared to its contents as they walked the few hundred yards to the Zombie Couple's camp.

Audra and Belinda eyed the scene. It was much like their own situation, but these two people had lost. Their fire had long died. A metal pot and other supplies were strewn about the ground. The camouflage green tent appeared in perfect condition except for a hole in the back that mice were using to transport things in and out. Mice meant more supplies hidden inside.

Had they both been capable, the sisters might have just waltzed into camp and killed the couple. However, Audra knew Belinda had a knack for freezing when life required her to stay in control of her body, and she could not handle the Zombie Couple by herself. The couple remained close together even in death. Audra could not kill one without being attacked by the other. She was much smaller than either of them and if she was bitten, who would care for Belinda? Audra decided Belinda would lure the pair into a slow moving single file. Audra would come from behind, kill the last in line, then kill the first before it had time to catch Belinda.

Near the perimeter of the camp, Belinda didn't dare shout to excite them. She just kicked about leaf debris to catch their attention. The man, in his flannel shirt and mussed thick-rimmed glasses, was closest. His heavy new work boots changed direction and headed for Belinda. The woman with tied back blond hair full of leaves saw her husband change direction in her peripheral vision. She turned and followed him. Belinda walked to keep her distance. Audra could hear Belinda whimpering. Poor Belinda. It was one thing to be scared of these things; it was another to be constantly asked to be bait.

Audra tip-toed through the camp to approach the blond woman from behind. The woman's linen shirt and leggings were moth-eaten and inappropriate for the weather. Audra took her dagger and plunged it into the back of the woman's skull. She crumpled onto the dry leaves, signaling her husband. He turned to his love and saw Audra still standing over her, her breath held. Before anything could be decided, another fall in the woods interrupted them. This one was unintended. Belinda cried out about her ankle as Zombie Husband flipped his head around. Audra exhaled relief before realizing Belinda was still rolling around on the ground, making no effort to escape.

Zombie Husband had closed almost all the distance between injured Belinda and himself before Audra arrived. He was too tall for Audra to reach from the ground. She jumped on his back, but they were too close to Belinda. Belinda froze in fright as the duo fell on top of her.

Audra had wrapped her legs around the zom on the way down and now was pinned between the two bodies. She used both hands to grab as much of his head and hair as she could and ripped it away from Belinda. She felt vertebra resist and then crack as she dislocated Zombie Husband's head. His back wrenched underneath her. The zombie made large bites into the air, barely missing Audra's fingers, his head internally decapitated and at a ninety-degree angle from his body. Belinda fainted.

Audra's dagger was lost in the leaves during the scuffle. She held his head with one hand and found her second dagger with the other. She let it cut through his forehead and his motions ended. A dead blond lay in a heap behind them. An unconscious blond lay underneath the flannel-clad zom. Audra, still piggy-backed, collapsed with exhaustion, burying her face in the camper's neck.

The Zombie Husband's putrid scent renewed her energy. Audra pulled her head up and inhaled the fresh air deeply. She leaned to one side and pulled the opposite leg out from underneath the heavy body. Freeing her second leg, she momentarily left the corpse on top of Belinda, who still had not revived on her own. Audra rested her head on her forearms, which were perched on her bent knees. That was much harder than she'd intended. And it would make every next encounter that much worse for Belinda.

Audra turned toward her sister. She braced her feet and rolled Zombie Husband off of Belinda, putting a foot on his face to yank out her dagger. She cleaned it on his pants and checked his pockets before pulling off his flannel shirt. The shirt was large enough for either of the girls to wear as an outer layer as the weather got cooler. Audra rolled it up and put it in her pack. The corpse remained in his undershirt with his farmer's tan showing. Audra pulled Belinda to a sitting position and let her rest against a tree. She could try to revive her now, but her breathing was steady and it would be easier to go through the supplies without her.

The tent looked glorious.

As she did the final sorting and replacing of items, Belinda stirred. Audra came over and crouched by her. She stroked her face and brushed the hair from it. Belinda did not open her eyes, but gave a content smile and murmured sweet sounds like a child waking up from a happy dream. Audra sat hip to hip with her, leaning against both Belinda and the tree.

"Good morning Beebs," Audra whispered.

Belinda made a bubbly noise.

"We got a tent, Beebs," she said as she crossed her legs in front and twiddled her thumbs, waiting for her sister to wake.

* * *

It took two days of running to get to the city of Macon. From there, you could take I-16 to Savannah or go west to Atlanta.

Some runners considered tagging on the outskirts of Atlanta, but the risks and costs were high. Finding a handful of requested bodies in a metropolitan area swarming with infected was not a good business or life plan, but Savannah was doable. Savannah was a port city, but still small. If they could get close enough, they could reach lots of supplies. And if not, there were plenty to tag whose last known location was "evacuating Savannah."

Audra knew most taggers had not been out this far. They stayed closer to town to minimize travel days, but finds were getting sparser and the search was becoming the largest expense in the tagging business.

I-16 had two lanes east and two lanes west. Westbound cars filled every lane and the median. People had remained in the unmoving traffic for days before they abandoned their cars looking for better opportunities. The cars had been long stripped of supplies, spare blankets, food, water, flashlights. All of that was gone. Audra and her family had been out here doing the looting once upon a time. But many of the cars did contain zombies. Were they people who had been bitten with the sense to isolate themselves? Or were they simply in denial that the traffic would clear and they would be on their way? Either way, a sprinkling of the cars had cooped up zombies without the fine motor skills to operate a door handle.

Easy pickings.

They approached a red sedan with an elderly lady lying on the back seat. Dwyn thought she was dead and started to the next car. Audra knew she just needed stimulation. Audra gave the car door a bump with the side of her hip. The little sedan jostled and the woman in her high-waisted khakis and knit sweater sprang up from the waist. Her eyes popped open and her face contorted as she realized food was about. She clawed at the window and Audra wondered why she had bothered. Grandma had already been abandoned once.

She was the first zombie in two days though. They had not seen a single one in the woods en route. Audra found it odd, but perhaps all the zoms in the area had followed people toward bigger cities or perhaps there was a corral. Lysent had hired "shepherds" to direct unwanted herds into contained areas to keep them from the towns.

With a tool from her pack, she popped the lock on the front passenger door like her mother had taught her. She nodded to Dwyn, who reached in and scraped Grandma's outstretched hand. DNA captured.

Name: Diana Lessing
Gender: Female
DOB: 2/2/1999
Status: No Inquiries

"Sorry, Grandma. Guess they should have just left you at the old folks' home."

Audra reached to place a yellow tag on Diana's ear. A pearl earring fell to the ground. Diana turned to bite in protest and Audra gave her a gentle punch, causing her dentures to fall. Audra had trouble placing the tag over her giggles. She locked the door behind her and hoped Grandma would calm down and return to her resting spot. At least her family would know her location if they ever inquired - in the red sedan where they had left her.

The second occupied car showed more promise. A teenage boy sat in the driver's seat wearing baggy jeans and a grungy t-shirt. In the emergency evacuation, he had found the time to style and gel his hair. He may have run away and was hiding out in cars when he was bitten. Maybe his family had thought of him after the cure was announced. He was worth a shot and good practice for Dwyn.

Audra munched on chicken jerky, trying to pass the time while Dwyn tried her tool on the lock. She coached him over a few steps but mostly let him flail about as she sat in the shade of the car. He put pressure on the window, trying to gain leverage. It cracked. Audra shook her head and laughed. Dwyn shrugged and used the tool to finish breaking the window.

Name: Link Culpepper
Gender: Male
DOB: 1/6/2063
Status: Inquired

"Audra, an inquiry!" said Dwyn, jumping up and down.

It was his first. He used Audra's reader per their agreement. Audra did not want to get her hopes up, though. An inquiry was far from credits in her pocket.

"OK, submit the find, tag him, and put him in here," she said as she stood up and popped the next car's lock in a fraction of Dwyn's time and effort. "We'll come back and get him if his parents want to pay up."

"Parents?"

"I doubt his high school sweetheart was dating him long enough to care, nor do I think she has cash. I'm betting on parents."

"Or, maybe a sibling?" Dwyn asked carefully.

"Yeah, maybe," Audra replied with a shortness that ended the conversation.

Dwyn unlocked the car door through the window and tempted Link outside. The teen's overenthusiastic desire for flesh and his poor processing skills tripped him over the car's door frame. He tumbled and scraped his face.

"Link, man, please remember to walk," requested Dwyn.

Audra's tendency to talk to the zombies had rubbed off on Dwyn. At first, Dwyn thought she was taunting them, but he admitted that her teasing respected their dangerous nature while still remembering that they were, somehow, still human.

Link pulled himself up and mumbled his distaste in his prey. He leaned forward too much, then over-corrected back. The drunk-looking teenager eventually made it over to the second car with Dwyn's luring.

This zombie could not chase people for a living. It was best if it stayed inside.

The door to the back seat was open and Audra stood on the other side of the car and banged on the window, trying to tempt Link with some girly flesh.

"I don't know if he's that discerning, Audra."

"Are you saying I'm lacking femininity?"

"Of course not."

Dwyn gave her a smile. His curly hair bounced with his movement and his blue eyes shone. He seemed to be enjoying their work. He pushed on the small of Link's back. Link landed in the car.

"Link, sweetie, you stay here. We're just going to run into the store," said Audra.

She was already looking for the next zombie. Who else was hiding in these cars? They could wrangle a tiny herd for a large payout worth their travel time. Audra looked to the endless line of cars. Maybe they would not have to travel the long miles to

Savannah to find what they needed.

Ten cars down yielded the find Audra was looking for, a young girl. Jackpot. Audra did not wait to let Dwyn practice on the lock. The girl with plaited hair was a poster child for tagging. Families were looking for lost children and missing spouses (unless they had already picked up another). Audra almost stabbed her with the reader.

Name: Unknown
Gender: Female
DOB: Unknown
Status: DNA not in database, no similar matches

"What does that even mean?" asked Dwyn.

"Well… I've never seen it, but her DNA isn't registered."

"How is that possible?"

"Guess she wasn't born in a hospital. They did that stuff routinely. She's off the grid."

"How will her family find her?"

He watched her inside the car. She didn't show interest in them. She was starving and tired.

"Similar matches would have been a parent or sibling, but she doesn't have any. Her whole family might be off the grid. If that's the case, they probably don't trust the corporation to find their daughter, anyway."

"Maybe she ran off and hid here after she got bit. I hope they find her out here," said Dwyn.

He pulled his pack up tighter and looked toward the forest.

"I'm sure they will," Audra lied.

Audra decided not to tell Dwyn that no one was truly *looking* anymore. Sure, her job was based on finding loved ones, but it was a haphazard way to do things. Family members would toss in a request and if someone happened to find the person, then arrangements were made. No one was leaving the comforts of their new townships to search for lost loved ones. This little girl and thousands of others were discarded and forgotten. Dwyn's ferocious optimism made her wonder. Would *he* show up on the DNA reader? Had *he* forgotten or been forgotten?

They saw nobody else for the next half mile and climbed on top of a tractor trailer to eat lunch. Audra lay out with an oat bar lazily in her hand. She felt safe up high and the heat coming off the metal felt good on her tired bones. Still, she knew she would regret falling asleep on the hard surface. Dwyn watched her with another goofy smile on his face as she fought her falling eyelids.

Audra spent a little longer on top of the trailer than she intended. They decided to run to the Savannah outskirts and camp there for the night. They could check vehicles on their way back and pick up Link, who Audra imagined was brooding in the car. In another life, she would be doing the same, not chasing zombies.

For a zombie chaser, Dwyn was becoming a talented runner, keeping pace with Audra as they pushed down the middle of the two lanes. Only a jutting side view mirror or mis-angled car slowed them down. Audra enjoyed the terrain change of flat asphalt and lack of thorns and brush. She inhaled with another right step forward and thought the slight breeze was what made the day's running perfect. Dwyn led by a little more than a car length.

Her inhalation took a sharp and unintended escape as a car door kicked open with great momentum. Audra ran into it full force and it did not give despite its hinges. Her head lurched forward above the car door while her torso remained behind her. Her body and head fell backward onto the asphalt in unison. Her head took an extra bounce. She heard a voice which faded into darkness.

* * *

When Audra's mind emerged, she felt cramped and on something structured and soft. After a few more moments, she realized she was lying in the back seat of a car. She did not believe a lot of time had passed. It was still daylight. She did not sit up but remained as still as possible. She did not want to alert her attacker she was awake as she assessed her pained body. Nothing appeared broken. The sound and pressure of her own pulse overtook any awareness of the back of her head. Audra imagined a big knot forming.

She tried to remember what had happened.

Someone had swung open the car door in front of her. They had braced it so it would not shut when she hit it. They'd known she was coming and trapped her.

Dwyn was up ahead.

Did they get Dwyn, too?

They had to have seen Dwyn. That meant he either escaped, or they had captured him, or worse. Audra tried to replay the visual moment she hit the car door. Was Dwyn also being hit by a door? Was there more than one assailant? She couldn't remember if she had seen Dwyn being attacked.

Audra closed her eyes to focus on a sound beyond the pounding in her head. She made out voices, two voices. They were arguing in hushed tones. Neither was Dwyn. Audra willed her pulse to quiet as she struggled to hear.

"Look, you can't mess with her. Corp said — only steal her pack — this isn't a level two op."

Audra's eyes widened. What the hell were they talking about? The other guy mumbled something that Audra could not make out.

"Dude. I ain't got time for this shit. Grab the pack and let's go. We gotta be gone."

Audra heard cursing, more grumbling, and someone kicking cars and debris. Her heart sank. She expected to hear a scuffle next and then for someone to come for her. She wanted to run, to jump out of the car and sprint for it. Her body ached. Would adrenaline let her run into the woods or would her head double her over? She was in no shape to outrun anyone, but at least she had the element of surprise, awake in the car. Audra stayed slumped with her eyes closed, despite what all her instinct screamed.

The noises faded. Audra was not sure how much time she let pass before she dared to open her eyes. It was still light out. Had she passed out? Were they still here? She could detect her pulse in the distant part of her head, birds outside, and nothing else. Five minutes passed, then ten. Were they gone? There was nothing left to do but to sit up and gather more information.

Her body felt bruised and heavy, but responsive. She planted her hands and straightened her elbows to pull her torso and head up. As she strained her neck to the window, pain seared forward from the knot on the back of her head and bubbles of light filled her vision. To gather herself, she attempted a deep breath, but her ribs popped in pain. When the stars left her, I-16 materialized in the window - cars everywhere and no one in sight. She took her time to position her back against the seat. The car felt like it was moving, but it was not. She was alone.

Were they gone for good? If they planned to keep her, one would have gone out and the other would have stood guard.

Instead, they had left her alone. Was Dwyn in another car? It was time to find out. Audra stumbled out of the sedan and into the road. A quick glance in both directions showed that her pack was nowhere to be found. She pursed her lips.

BANG BANG!

Audra's body dropped to the asphalt without her permission, her eyes spread wide. They had come back for her. She wasn't safe.

BANG BANG!

Audra came to her senses. The sound was coming from a car up ahead. She called out and recognized Dwyn's voice. She raced to the muffled sound and popped the trunk that hid it. Dwyn barely sat up before Audra fell into his arms.

"Thank God, you're alive," she said in between the tears that overcame her.

All the fear bubbled up and threw Audra over. It threw her and wrecked her, much to her surprise. In just a few short moments, she composed herself. She let Dwyn emerge from the car trunk where he knelt. He struggled to swing his legs over the side, perhaps in as much pain as Audra.

"Do you remember what happened?" she asked.

He leaned up against the bumper and looked at a distant spot on the ground, willing his memories to form.

"I heard you hit something… I turned around and saw the car door. I ran toward it and got pushed from behind."

"Yeah, there were two of them."

"We fought, but I was already on the ground. He must have knocked me out and shoved me in the trunk. Are you OK?" he asked, suddenly realizing that he did not know what happened after that point. Anything could have happened.

Audra nodded, "I'm fine. They shoved me in the car. Stole

our packs."

"Do you know who they were?"

"I overheard one of them say they were from the corporation…" said Audra grimly, not providing all the information she heard. "They made it sound like it was a planned attack by Lysent. Would they do something like that?"

"You tell me, Audra. You're the one who works with them. Maybe they thought you were getting too far in your contract. You found Link pretty quickly after Randy."

Audra stayed silent. But how did they know where she was?

The reader. It sent her location every time she ran DNA. They knew she was running along I-16. She was predictable.

The two sat and leaned partially against the car's back tire and partially against each other. They looked up and down the road, surveying their predicament. A small sigh escaped Audra's lungs. That pack was her livelihood. Her tent, her food, the bit of money she had left, her spare clothes, her cooking pot, her photos of her family at Disney World and another one by the Christmas tree. Soon she would have to stand up and fight to survive, but for a moment she mourned for what she had lost.

The Christmas tree and the amusement park were gone. And now, their photographic evidence was gone, too. She stood as the last vessel that could recall those memories. And if Lysent prevented her from waking up her sister, they would fade forever.

Anger set in. And she stood up.

CHAPTER SIX

Audra smiled over the simmering pot. She caught a rabbit and had stretched it over three meals supplementing it with mushrooms and wild onions. As she scooped it into their tin cups, Belinda did not thank her for once again providing for her. Audra noticed Belinda eat the vegetables around the meat.

"I'm going for a walk. I'll finish on the way." Belinda was never a good liar.

She had not eaten any of the rabbit in the last three days. Audra watched her walk into the woods in the dusky light, ignoring her temptation to follow her. How would Belinda grow if Audra was always right over her shoulder? She needed space.

And so did Audra. She appreciated the few moments alone. Belinda required constant comforting, not to mention help to stay alive and fed. She had trouble accepting her new life. When can we go back to the city? When can I sleep in a real bed? Belinda was not content with survival. She wanted more.

A cry broke through the woods.

Audra jumped over the fire and into the woods where she

had seen her sister disappear. Belinda wailed again and Audra adjusted the trajectory of her sprint. Not knowing what she would find, she pulled out her dagger. The woods seemed to have become so much darker in the few minutes' gap between thinking it was OK for Belinda to wander and now fearing for her. She should have kept a better watch on her. This was her fault.

Audra spotted Belinda underneath a small outcropping and stopped when she realized that Belinda was not crying for help. Belinda knelt over a bloodied mass, crying over the animal she had been feeding. This was where Audra's rabbit had been going.

Belinda's back was to her and it felt, to their new world. Audra stood at a distance deciding whether she should leave Belinda to mourn or provide help. However, something else began to encroach.

"Belinda! Zombie!"

The animal blood mingled on his face and clothing. The zombie responsible for the death had returned. Audra ran toward them but stopped in her tracks as Belinda turned, reared up, and roared. Belinda grabbed her whittling knife from her belt and sprinted toward the shambler. Audra's surprise wore off, but she remained back to observe. Belinda needed to learn combat.

"You killed them!" she shouted, shaking with anger as she came down on it.

It was on the ground before it could understand what was happening. Belinda was on top, screaming, stabbing and stabbing. What she did not have in accuracy, she made up for in enthusiasm. Eventually, the zombie stopped moving and Belinda grew tired. She sat in the leaves with her legs in front of her, panting to catch her breath.

Perhaps Belinda would get the hang of this after all.

After a few minutes, Belinda went back to the mama dog and her dead pups. She mourned for them like she mourned for all lost life.

* * *

Audra and Dwyn kept to I-16. It was a direct path and cars were available for shelter anytime they needed it. But, foraging for food and keeping water was difficult, and even Audra was forced to slow down. From I-16, they reached the rail line and a week later, arrived on Vesna's doorstep with nothing to their names. Vesna fed them immediately. Despite Vesna's secondary agenda, Audra struggled to name another who would have been as generous. Maybe Rosie if they had ever had any dealings outside the corporation. Rosie tried to look out for her. Or so she thought. Did Rosie know what was planned for her? Was she letting it happen? There was obvious truth in Vesna's speech, but how much? Audra always felt uneasy about leaving her sister in their care, but now fear crept in. If they hired people to hurt their own contractors, how safe was her sister?

The next morning, she arrived in the second township that held Lysent and her sister. Lysent charged indentured taggers for family visits, citing transportation and safety concerns to justify the fees. She had last seen her sister in July - Belinda's birthday. She was in no position to confront Lysent, nor ready to reveal what she knew, but she needed to make sure her sister was all right.

Audra waved to Clyde, who was wheeling a body outside the township fences to be buried. With a shake of his head, he confirmed it wasn't a zom Audra had known, but it was a reminder that she was running out of time.

As always, Rosie greeted her from the desk. Audra tried to decipher whether there was a hint of surprise in the receptionist's eyes. She could not tell.

"I want to see my sister."

"Sure, the usual fee will apply. Did you… bring in a zombie?" Rosie asked, riffling through her paperwork for maybe a communication she had missed.

"No. My reader was stolen. I need a new one."

Rosie stopped rummaging through papers and looked up at her. Her eyebrows came together and wrinkled with worry. She looked back to her papers as if she thought better of whatever she might have said.

"Sure, the usual fee will apply…" as she rummaged through papers again.

Rosie located Audra's thick folder in the cabinet and matched it up against the pricing sheet she found on the desk. Her eyes furrowed when she saw some of the recent notes. Audra tried to catch a peek, but the papers were strategically positioned.

"You've already lost a reader. This one will cost double."

Audra gave a puzzled look.

"I've never lost a reader. Look again."

"Sorry Audra, it says you lost one last year. Serial number 23."

"I never had 23. Mine was 9."

The receptionist showed signs of impatience.

"Well, bring back your reader and we will read the number on it."

Audra glared at Rosie. They were typically cordial, but Rosie's trust in her sloppy paperwork annoyed Audra. And she wanted to know what was written in her chart that suddenly made her down two readers. Every step back she encountered with Lysent flashed through her mind. Had everything been perfectly balanced to leave her screwed without her realizing?

Audra sighed.

"What is my account at?"

"With the THIRD reader, the visit today, and the month's rent since you were last here… 1.8 million credits. 1.2 if you bring back the reader this time."

How could she be in worse shape than when she walked in with Belinda? She had been working for years. Rosie distracted herself by pushing paperwork around on her desk.

"Fine. Let me see my sister."

"Sure, give us an hour and we will be ready."

An hour later, Clyde escorted Audra farther onto the campus, which looked something in between a hospital and a prison. Clyde had aged more than the three years they had known each other. He had lost muscle mass, leaving him as thin as any other Lysent office worker. But Audra knew he was deceptively strong. If a zombie had crossed the front plaza, Clyde had manhandled it. He escorted both claimed and collateral zoms around the property. He wore his white robe which was not commensurate with his job, but with his status. Audra had never questioned it, but now she questioned everything. Why did they have time to be clean and sparkly? Where did they get such nice fabric when she only had the shirt on her back?

A man in a white lab coat was waiting for Clyde and Audra in the front lobby.

"This way," he said without greeting as he turned down the hall.

Audra waved her goodbye to Clyde as she followed, feeling like a kid in trouble at school. This was "the hotel" where zoms were stored and awakened. The windowed front rooms showed the rich their loved ones' accommodations. Zoms often occupied the rooms, "in holding" to be awakened. Audra swore she saw repeats though as if they were on rotation. Audra had ignored it, just as she had ignored the fact she had never met a success story from the indentured tagging program. She had overlooked a lot in the process of helping her sister.

Her escort opened the door to the visitation room. Audra looked farther down the hall before entering. She had once asked for a tour but was told it would stress out the "guests." They reported the scientists were trained to keep the guests perfectly calm and healthy. Audra wondered what it looked like back there. How many zoms? How much space did Belinda have?

"Just come out when you are ready," he prompted.

Floor to ceiling acrylic glass split the white sterile room in half. Drilled holes at the top and bottom of the glass equalized the air pressure. On her side, a white pine chair sat for her convenience. On the other side, stood an almost stranger in a white jumpsuit with thinning hair and a sallow complexion. She stared at one of the opaque side walls, unmoving. Audra noticed less and less movement from her sister with each visit. Was it because she was left in the dark between visits? Maybe the hour was to help her adjust to the light of the room.

Audra walked forward until her body leaned against the glass. She used her full palm to tap twice on the surface. Belinda's blond head turned slowly toward the noise. She stood for a moment looking at the frozen image of Audra. Belinda appeared intact but empty.

"Hi, Belinda."

Belinda's jaw dropped and her body pivoted. She walked with a small stagger, each step slow and shuffling. Audra remained still with her hand on the glass and watched as her sister came to meet her. She was the same height. They had the same cheekbones, but even in ruin, Belinda's beauty was undeniable. Belinda's mouth opened wide to capture Audra's. On close inspection, Audra noticed Belinda's skin drooped on her cheekbones.

"I'm sorry you're still in here."

Belinda's bare feet kept tapping the bottom of the wall as she continued her walk. Audra looked down at her feet. They were clean and unbruised. Were the baseboards in her room padded? Did she have a room at all? Audra had handed over Belinda to Lysent, burying herself in debt. She was not sure if they had started the epidemic, but they had started this lie. Audra wished she had never approached them.

Belinda followed Audra as she walked along the room to one corner. Audra knelt down and stuck her knife into one of the holes. Careful to avoid Belinda, she sawed at it to test its durability. It gave way, but slowly. Audra would need another tool to cut enough acrylic to access her sister, but at least it was an option.

Belinda dropped down to her level.

"I promise I'll make it right," Audra whispered.

Audra heard the door behind her swing open. Her fingertips guided her knife up her sleeve as she turned on her heels to look. She was shocked to see Larange Greenly standing there, two guards on either side. Had she set off a silent alarm? With no other option, she shot a surprised and annoyed look at the person interrupting family time.

"I am sorry to bother you, Miss Audra. I heard you were here, visiting your sister. How is she?"

Audra's anger simmered in her chest above her heart and threatened to overflow from her collarbone. In truth, Audra did not know how her sister was doing. They were on opposite sides of acrylic. And on this side, Audra wondered, for the first time, if she should incite change with her knife hidden in her sleeve and the leader at arm's reach. Audra imagined that was why she was escorted by guards even within her own walls.

"You should know how she's doing. You're the one in charge of this shin-dig."

Why was Greenly bothering her now? They had not met since she'd asked to be a tagger those years ago. Greenly had better things to do than to confront an indentured tagger, didn't she? The audacity overwhelmed her.

"In fact," Audra continued, "you've been in charge from the start, so I've heard, anyway. I was just a child when this virus broke out. Seems odd that such a big biomedical, communications, blah blah blah company dutied to fight the virus as it swept the nation could still land on top at the end."

Audra stared Greenly down as she spoke and saw her eyes dodge hers almost imperceptibly. Audra searched her face for the truth, but the flinch disappeared as Greenly retorted.

"From your current status, it seems, my dear, that you have no idea how to manage your own personal finances, much less know what big business is all about. I heard you've lost another of our readers. Those are very valuable. Something will have to be done if your account continues further in the red."

Greenly's eyes moved from Audra to the girl behind the glass, pointedly. Her face withered into disgust at the presence of her charge.

"I think I know exactly what this big business is about."

* * *

A few blocks away from the corporation campus, Dwyn approached her with two oat bars in his hand. He was anxious to feed her again. They had gotten quite weak during their time out. Audra waved him off as she picked up speed and ran out of the village. Lysent was watching her. And while they already knew Dwyn tagged with her, she didn't want them to know how close they had gotten. Audra didn't even like how close they had gotten. But she didn't have time to think about that. She needed to wrap her mind around meeting Greenly. A drink was tempting, but she had no money to her name. So instead, she went for a run. There was no better place to think than on a run.

The runner stayed on the well-traveled path. The soft pounding of her feet ushered her thoughts. It was clear the indentured path would never work. Greenly would never let her or her sister out of the contract. She was too valuable as a tagger and Belinda was her motivation. In a world of uncontrollable zombies, Greenly settled for power over individuals. Greenly had made that clear by arriving in person to the visitation room. She used Belinda, but Audra could use Belinda, too. Surviving the week to find her sister still alive, gave her a new sense of urgency. She had tagged for three years now. If she wanted their lives back, she was going to have to fight for it. Vesna's group was a new opportunity and for now, her best bet.

As if her decision dictated the run, she found herself back near the village gate. There, Dwyn waited. He hadn't waited to eat though.

"How is Belinda?" he asked as he handed Audra a half-eaten bar.

Out of sight of the village, they walked farther away from possible ears.

"She looked OK. You guys are right, though. That place is not what it seems."

She described her encounter to Dwyn.

"Why is Greenly suddenly interested in you?"

Audra shrugged her shoulders. Greenly had seemed amused when Audra had arrived a rail-thin girl accompanying her infected sister, asking to go on dangerous missions for the chance to wake her up. She had gone through the ranks of taggers, and now, as Audra saw it, often cut down by the corporation when her own failures did not see an end to it. Her stomach boiled with the revelation. She handed back the oat bar and they ran to Vesna's village. She needed to talk with her.

The open-air market housed many vendors, but Vesna ran a Lysent-sponsored supply shop which carried hard-to-find items. Rather than drag everything in and out of the market, Vesna ran her shop. Dwyn explained Vesna had to do paperwork on any unusual purchases, like laboratory equipment or big weapons, but otherwise, it put her in a great position to supply a rebellion.

They entered the little cottage on the main drag. Equipment for camping, farming, and hunting was stacked along the walls and on the shelves. Vesna was the only occupant.

"How is your sister?" Vesna asked as she popped her head out from under the front counter.

Dwyn's and Vesna's concern for her sister surprised Audra. Few in the world inquired about her and her sister's life. Audra answered, not mentioning Greenly's visit. Dwyn noticed but did not interrupt. Audra was not there to share but to gather information. Just because she was not on Lysent's side, did not mean she should default to Vesna's.

"Where are you from? What did you do before?" Audra asked.

If Vesna was taken aback by the personal question, she did not show it. Audra was showing interest in their group. It was a good thing. Vesna's face dimmed as she recalled her prior life.

"I was a mother and an attorney. I lived in what used to be North Carolina with my family. They are all gone now. Lysent recommended we burn all the bodies and the state government complied."

With every syllable addressing Lysent, her shoulders hunched more in anger.

"I've hated them from the start. I think they started all of this. As a lawyer, I was involved in a few suits against them. I know what they are about."

Audra recognized a strong ally with hatred coursing through her veins. While they had dissimilar goals, they had a common enemy and the same strong thread of motivation. They were both the last of their families. If all of Lysent fell, it would be the last of that "family" as well. She cut the interrogation short.

"I will help if you help retrieve my sister and cure her."

Vesna nodded, her face almost grim with seriousness. Her anger still intense. But Dwyn broke into a large grin.

"Hand over your reader. Let's open it up," commanded Vesna.

Audra jerked back. She had just gone down the hole another 0.6 million credits to get this damn reader. She didn't even have a backpack to put it in. Now her new leader wanted to break it open?

"I'll be careful. Readers send out your GPS signal when you submit a find, but we need to make sure they did not doctor this one to track your movements."

Audra sighed but gave her the device. Vesna pulled out a screwdriver and carefully pried it apart. Vesna looked it over and seemed satisfied.

"It's clean. It will only transmit your location when you read DNA and submit it."

"So, I still have to be careful where I submit DNA. They will know where I am and possibly guess where I'm going."

"Yes, that's correct, but we also can use that to our advantage. Eat up, and you can sleep here tonight. Dwyn will give you details of your first mission. You'll get supplies tomorrow."

"I'd rather sleep in a tent. Do you have a tent I could borrow?"

"If you want to sleep in a tent, you might as well resupply now. Take what you need." Vesna swept her hand to gesture at the entire store.

Audra looked over at the shelves of equipment. Working with Vesna was a good choice. She picked up the lightest pack she could find and layered it with a small tent, blanket, a light cooking pot, a canteen, and food. Audra had never collected so many things at once. She had worked hard for every piece of equipment in her pack, especially that tent. Audra tested the weight of the pack. Some of the things were heavier than she desired but necessary to have.

As Audra gave her thanks and started to leave, Vesna turned to Dwyn.

"Oh and see that she does not get into trouble."

Dwyn did not acknowledge the command. Audra let out a "humph" of disapproval but did not pick a fight, since she had an entire pack of gifts. It appeared her recruitment did little to soften Vesna's directions.

The pair walked out and into the late sunshine. Dwyn tilted his head to look at his partner, whose mind had already wandered to the nearest moonshiner's hideout, around the corner on a dusty road. The shiner's specialty was "blue moon corn," but Audra only cared about the alcohol content. Perhaps she could work for a few drinks?

Dwyn interrupted her thoughts without confronting their contents.

"Want to go for a test run with our new packs?"

CHAPTER SEVEN

It was not quite dawn when Dwyn stuck his head into Audra's tent.

"They are here."

"Have them be here later. It's not even light out."

"They're… an enthusiastic bunch."

Dwyn had spoken the truth. When Audra stumbled out, a hand thrust itself into her personal space as an engineer greeted the sleepy woman.

"It is such a pleasure to meet you! We've been waiting weeks to move onto the next phase in the development. I'm Ryder, by the way. We can't work in the village anymore without risking being detected," the young woman with spiked brown hair chattered on as Audra mustered the patience.

Ryder's two partners stood back. One gave a little wave, but neither looked keen to be outside the fences. Ryder introduced them. Ziv had long hair and a full beard that took over much of his thin frame. Satomi looked younger than Ryder if that was possible. Her dark hair shimmered in the sunlight as she brushed it out of her face nervously. Audra noticed Dwyn's grin was larger and goofier this morning.

Audra sighed when she looked past the trio to their four large wagons of stuff they would take to the laboratory.

"You can't transport all of this in one trip," Audra said with an air of impatience.

This trip would be a long one if she was going to pull somebody else's wagon of unneeded crap. Ryder smiled.

"Yes, I guess we have a lot of equipment, but..." Ryder said, pulling out a remote with joysticks on it, "all the wagons are solar powered and remote controlled. As long as we stay on the road, it shouldn't be too hard for the wagons to match our pace."

Audra's eyebrows rose as one of the carts picked up speed and traveled down the road.

"Impressive," said Audra.

Here she was with nothing to her name, and this girl was making solar powered motor vehicles.

"...I had some time while we were waiting for you guys," said Ryder with a shrug.

Audra stepped back and addressed the group.

"OK, listen up. Dwyn and I will take turns taking point, so we don't stumble into any herds or corrals. The other will stay close to the group to guard against lateral movements from zoms and to protect our backside. I don't know how much experience you have with zombies but stay away from the end that bites. They are attracted to loud sounds, bright visual stimuli, and human smells. Please avoid being those things."

"Yes," said Satomi, "those are all housed in the lower brain."

Knowing anatomy was not the same as being able to survive a zom attack, but Audra nodded. At least Satomi and Ryder were engaging in what she was saying. That was a good sign. Ziv just shuffled from foot to foot. Maybe he would get eaten.

Ryder thanked Audra, and they were soon on their way. Months ago, Dwyn had located the laboratory through old paperwork and maps. He had visited, but there were too many zombies for him to clear out on his own. The lab was thirty miles down the highway, and then ten miles off. Dwyn would explain the situation at the lab en route.

Boredom set in for the new explorers. Ziv was the loudest, complaining about blisters after just two hours. Audra was not sure how hard to push them. She did not want to stress them, but she also did not want to spend the rest of her life walking forty miles. Audra could do that in a day and a half, at leisure. This was painfully slower than leisurely pace and occasionally interrupted by a cart flipping and tossing all its contents. She tried to distance everyone from their displeasure, including her own, by learning more about the new team.

Ryder had worked with the antidote at Lysent. Her parents had been Lysent scientists, and she was recruited at a young age. No one at Lysent had been able to tell her how the antidote was developed. It just existed. When she'd learned that she was just replicating limited batches of doses without work to advance their knowledge or better help the country, she had looked for ways to leave.

Ziv had taught biochemistry at a local college but was quick to point out that he had little practical experience. He offered no information on what he had been doing since. Audra gathered it was not much. He was not pleasant to talk to, so Audra did not try.

Satomi was about as much of a medical student as people could be now. She had studied under a traditionally taught doctor and had pored over medical textbooks. More than the practical day-to-day, she learned epidemiology and immunology. Satomi was interested in how the virus spread and methods of eradication. How the corporation had not picked her up yet was a curiosity to Audra. Ryder reported the recruitment would have come shortly.

The group walked eight miles before they decided that a dinner break was in order. Audra suggested they set up camp and start back out in the morning. It would be best to keep the explorers rested. Perhaps renewed energy and enthusiasm would compensate for their lack of experience. Audra doubted it.

When Ziv's head emerged from his tent the next morning, his eyes darted left and right before he stepped out. He surveyed the woods despite everyone already being out and about. With no dangers in sight, he finished with a glare directed at Audra.

Audra raised her eyebrows in amusement.

"Yes?" she offered.

"This is ridiculous. You should have cleared the path, the lab, and then come to get us. You're unnecessarily risking our lives. We're very valuable. We're scientists."

His answer was quick, something he had been stewing on for most of the night.

Audra looked around to see if anyone agreed. Satomi seemed to become smaller, wishing to avoid the conflict. Ryder was about to dismiss him in her cheery, talkative way, but Audra interrupted.

"All lives are valuable, Ziv. The sooner we get you to the laboratory, the sooner you can help them… all."

Ziv huffed and retreated into his tent. This was the person she would be relying on to save her sister?

"I'm sorry," said Ryder, apologizing for him. "Of course we believe everyone is worth saving and that there is still a sense of urgency after all these years. We're just not used to being… out here. It's a little scary. I don't think Ziv has ever been outside the township. I just left my job at Lysent. We're just new to all of this."

Breakfast was silent after the outburst, except for Ryder's sporadic attempts to boost morale. She bounced around enthusiastically, but it didn't hide the fact they were all tired and sore.

They got a later start than Audra had imagined. Everything seemed to take disproportionately longer with scientists in tow. And Audra could only listen to their complaints so long. When she tired of them, she would charge ahead and Dwyn would stay with the crew, helping to balance things on the cart, encouraging tired and blistered feet, and making sure nobody got lost.

It took seven days to get to the laboratory. Seven long days. Thankfully it did not rain. Audra thought that would have been the end of the scientists' morale. All of their water repellent gear would have been used to cover the sensitive equipment, leaving the group to soak in the rain. The scientific trio cheered when they reached the industrial park, surrounded by tall chain-link fences topped with barbed wire. Audra and Dwyn motioned for them to be quiet. They still had to clear out the place and it would not help to get the zombies riled up before they could establish a plan.

* * *

Dwyn and Audra escorted the scientists out of visual sight of the park and had them set up camp. They were getting much better at it. At least scientists were fast learners. Dwyn and Audra walked a large perimeter around the camp to verify that the crew would be safe before scouting out the park. Dwyn repeated the information he had gleaned from his last trip, words he had recited to her many times already. Audra did not quiet him; she knew he was nervous. He had seen almost a dozen within the fences, outside the buildings. The laboratory was along the east side of the industrial park, close to the fence. Looking through the windows, he had seen several zombies moving around inside, but did not have an exact count. It was too much for one person, especially with Dwyn's skill set when he last came.

They circled around the park until they found the entrance with just a traffic arm bar across the threshold. A quick inspection showed a chain-link fence that could be pulled closed. They would leave it open for now, in case they needed a speedy escape. The dusty road that led to it must lead to the highway, the opposite direction from town.

They both had daggers in their hands and spare ones in their boots. Dwyn's right leg shook in nervous excitement like it wanted to tap the ground, but it did not for fear of making noise. Audra's leg shook too from lack of cash and moonshine as of late. She was glad to reach the pinnacle of their mission. Vesna had agreed to pay her afterward.

"Ready?" asked Dwyn.

Audra just gave a grin, ducked under the arm, and ran to the first building. Dwyn gave chase to get ahead. They wrapped around the building and Dwyn turned the corner to look. He motioned that there were two within view. Audra took the right one. Dwyn took the left. Quick motion with their knives let two fall.

The front side of the park was now clear. Now to pick a building to be their zombie pen. A quick peek inside the front office showed four in there. The front office it was. They would corral them all in there for a pool of experimental subjects.

Audra moved to the next building and tested the door. It was unlocked. A woman wearing a long dress, fake pearls, and an administrative-appropriate hairstyle greeted her at the door.

Audra apologized for not having an appointment.

She baited her outside and into the front office. Dwyn pushed her farther in and closed the door with a smile on his face. While he had less experience killing, he had learned great handling skills.

Not all were as demure as the assistant. Some zombies were faster and required the two to run and even sometimes sprint. It was difficult to tell who would be fast. Audra knew if she was ever bitten, she would be damn fast. By midday, they reached the laboratory. A quick peek inside the door showed more occupants than in the other buildings combined. There were at least twenty. What was this isolated group doing? Audra and Dwyn both needed more energy to tackle the group. They would come back after lunch.

With no screams heard from the camp, Audra did not worry. They were met with a roaring fire, treated water, and a rotating nap schedule in the pop up tents. The scientists had taken up guard to watch for biters. They did well although the fire was a little large. Audra gave them a pass - this part of the country seemed abandoned, the road unkempt and the laboratory forgotten.

"How many subjects will you need?" asked Audra.

She used her jaw to tear off a particularly tough piece of jerky.

"It really depends, but we'd like to keep them all alive. Why? Are there a lot in the industrial park?" asked Ryder.

"We've corralled about twenty, but the laboratory has at least that many."

Audra looked Ryder straight in the eye, letting her jerky hand fall to her hip.

"I need to ask you something," Audra said.

"Yes?"

"How did you know this laboratory was here? Why is it full of people?"

No answer from Ryder. Satomi, who usually leaned toward silence, spoke up for Ryder.

"Ziv worked with a group in there, studying the infected. It went bad."

She walked to her tent, knowing the rest of the conversation did not need her. Everyone turned to Ziv.

"I had just started there. None of that was under my control," Ziv retorted.

"You were experimenting with… people?" asked Dwyn.

Ziv's head hung low and his long hair covered his quiet face. What Audra had already realized, suddenly came to Dwyn.

"Did everyone get infected but you?" asked Dwyn with some innocence left in his voice, but gradually doing the math in his head.

Ziv was slow to answer. Audra rolled her eyes. She did not want to listen to the sad story he was about to draw up. She was instead concerned about more pertinent information that he had kept from them.

"How many are there?"

"Fifteen scientists, three original infected. Eighteen total."

"How many rooms are there? Is anybody locked up? Are the doors locked? Are there other exits?" Audra spouted off questions.

Ziv seemed relieved that some of his secrets had been

revealed. He answered her questions as well as he could. Audra tried to hide her anger. If they had not come back for lunch, they would have been clearing the laboratory without this information, information that could save their lives.

After she gleaned what she needed, she and Dwyn headed back. A look inside the lab showed sallow men and women in white lab coats splattered with blood, but otherwise clean. Besides some knocked over beakers and Erlenmeyer flasks and liquid on the floor, the laboratory was in fairly good shape, too.

They approached the front door, which would open into the lobby. It was locked, just as Ziv shared. Although Audra had pulled a lot of information from Ziv, she still did not fully trust it. The infected group, one survivor, and one locked door revealed his character. She needed to trust her own instincts.

And here, her first chance performed a hip-heavy walk toward her, clad in a white lab coat with a large blood stain on the hanging sleeve as if her arm had retreated farther into the lab coat for protection. Audra grabbed the hanging sleeve and pulled on the other to tie it into a faux strait-jacket. Dwyn caught sight of Audra's doing as the zom ping-ponged through the door frame. He rolled his eyes. Dwyn bear hugged it from behind, securing the arms low on the hips, and shuffled to the front building. He called back to Audra to close the door and wait for him, but Audra had already slipped inside.

The dark wood panels on the wall gave a distinctly dated and untouched vibe. Paneling like that was long gone, often used as firewood or reinforcement. On the front desk, a phone sat with many lines unblinking and papers strewn, or thoughtfully organized if you consulted Rosie. A couch, soon to be fought over, shared its space with fading magazines - fodder for future sleepless nights. The rest of the room was empty. Audra opened the interior door and the warm colors of the front gave way to the more classic white tile and counter tops of a lab. Geeky zombies bounced from counter to counter, no longer able to perform their research.

Audra considered the knowledge lost in the minds here; knowledge seemed in short supply now. They should be saved if she could help it. One came running to her and grabbed at her neck. She sunk her dagger into it. Well, if they had such great minds, they wouldn't have gotten infected.

Dwyn joined her outside the doorway, saw the downed zombie, and scolded Audra playfully with his eyes. Audra smiled slyly, which received a joking push in return. It was then she realized he was close enough for her to feel his breath on her ear, moving the wisps of hair along her neck. Her lack of movement signaled Dwyn. He backed off, but a second adrenaline pulsed through her body as they entered the laboratory.

Audra and Dwyn returned late into the evening. The campfire had been calmed down a great deal more, despite Audra's silence on the matter. With the darkness of the night and their protectors busy on the other side of the fence, they did little to draw attention to themselves. Audra and Dwyn leaned up against a log, kicked off their boots, and breathed. They had done well. As their reward, the scientists gifted the two with freeze-dried meals. The reconstituted hash browns and chicken gave blessed variety from the jerky and oat bars that filled their lives.

Her feast was interrupted by the scientists' chatter about their future endeavors. Their casual talk of human experimentation frightened Audra. It seemed foreign and cold. Ryder noticed Audra's trepidation and stepped outside her scientific circle to comfort.

"We get that they are real people and what we're doing is of consequence, but it's better for the process if we coldly analyze. And honestly, burying ourselves in our work allows us to distance ourselves from the event and from dwelling on how it has personally impacted us. It's our way of coping and hopefully it also eventually helps others."

Audra could understand. Her escape was not science - it was running. The comfort of the repetition, the skill, it let her forget that the world was crumbling down around them.

With a full belly and a greater understanding, Audra leaned against Dwyn's shoulder and stared into the fire's sparks. Even if she now went back to tagging in the morning, she did feel secretly accomplished for helping this group under Lysent's nose. And she was actually enjoying their company. They weren't like the other villagers, content in their shell of existence. They and Belinda had that in common. And if they figured out how to create an antidote, Audra's Belinda would be the first in line.

The next morning, the scientists were up bright and early to move into their new laboratory. Audra showed them how to operate the front gate and gave them some tips on how to avoid being seen by people passing on the road. They had trouble listening. Even Ziv was excited to restock the laboratory and go back to their happy science lives. After a quick inventory, Audra was handed a letter for Vesna requesting additional supplies.

Audra was six miles out before her body and her mind realized she was running. Away from the chatter of the scientists, she sensed the solitude even with Dwyn on her tail.

Just the rustling of the debris beneath her, the scratching on her pant legs by the brush, and the speckling of the sun on her face. Running seemed to be her natural pace. Her body which seemed awkward and small when near others, felt most natural in movement, running in the woods.

While Dwyn had much improved, Audra still outran him in the longest distances, but Audra did seem exceptional in that regard. Dwyn slowed to walk after twenty miles. Audra scolded him for not eating enough to get through the four-hour mark. Dwyn rolled his eyes.

"I'll meet you up there," he conceded.

Audra ran the forty miles back to the township. It was late in the evening, but Vesna was there to receive her. She perused the letter as Audra unpacked items she did not need. Vesna reluctantly counted out the money she'd promised Audra.

"Are you sure you don't want to stay here for the night?" asked Vesna.

Audra heard the judgment in her voice. She did not know Vesna well enough to wait for Dwyn in her company. With her payout in her pocket, she said her good night.

Audra stepped out into the cool air. She was proud of her work. Food and sleep could be enough after the long run. Maybe she wouldn't drink tonight.

A drink, just one, would be nice.

She shouldn't.

An odd but distinct odor wafted to her. Yelling broke out into the night. She turned the corner toward the commotion and saw a small stable on fire within the confines of the township. There were people running to help. Audra ran to help too, but then the flames licked up. She froze.

CHAPTER EIGHT

Belinda jumped up and down, clapping her hands. Her eyes squinted with her large smile. Audra had just given her the all-clear after searching the tiny wood cabin and finding no zombies or humans within. Zoms were easy, humans were not. Audra kept them clear of people, much to Belinda's loneliness. There was only so much protection Audra could provide and people were unpredictable. But the horizontal surfaces of the cabin had a short layer of dust, everything creaked, and there was no food to be found. Audra almost jumped off the stoop to get out of Belinda's way as she stormed the place. Belinda ran circles around the small cabin, stomping inside.

"It's like Christmas, Audra! Do you think it's Christmas time?"

Audra looked out the grimy window for reference, but could not see much. It had been cold for about a month. There was no snow in southern Georgia. Could be Christmas, for all they knew.

They would possibly find a well outside, but the kitchen had been destroyed. The sink had fallen through the cabinets, all the cabinet doors were off their hinges as if someone had opened them in search of food, and they had rotted off their hinges by their own weight from being open for so long. The place was full of mildew and cobwebs. As awful as it was, it had been Belinda's dream for months. Tears of joy found the corners of Audra's eyes. This place was dangerous. Had she been on her own, she would not stay here. It was safer to camp in non-permanent structures, moving from place to place. But she'd risk it for Belinda. Belinda needed this rotting two-room cabin.

A scream from the other room pierced Audra's heart with fear. She followed Belinda's earlier march, pulling out her dagger. She recalled all the spaces in the bedroom. What had Belinda uncovered?

A bed.

Belinda fell backward onto the mattress and spread out her arms and legs. It fit her entire body. Belinda had not seen a bed since they'd evacuated their homes and gone to the community "safe" house where she and Audra had shared a cot. Belinda hated it then, but she had since stated she missed it when the uneven earth poked at her sore body.

"Come on, Audra! Come sleep with me!"

That night, they curled up together in the bed. It emanated funk, but it was so soft and so big. Belinda nuzzled up against Audra's neck. So many years ago this bed would have been in their nightmares, little mouse holes from their nesting and removal of stuffing, cockroach eggs, and proof of other vermin. But none of those things could worsen their condition now. They slept with mice and bugs in warehouses and even in cars. At least now this thing was soft and actually meant to be a bed. Audra pulled the surrounding blankets tighter and fell asleep with her sister in her arms.

She woke up without Belinda by her side. The spot next to her felt cool to the touch. Audra reveled in being in a real bed, stretching her arms above her head and her legs below. The grime in the window was lighter than before. The sun must be up. Audra's socked feet touched the dusty floor. As she stood up, the floor gave a little creak.

"Belinda?" Audra asked toward the other room.

It was odd not to have her by her side.

"Come in here!" said Belinda cheerfully.

Audra felt surprised to hear sleepy-head Belinda so energetic in the morning. She shuffled into the front room to find Belinda holding up a small three-foot fir tree. It leaned dangerously far as Belinda had not neatened the cut edge on the bottom. Underneath it lay a basket of winter berries and a small wooden cardinal that Belinda had been whittling during their long hours in the woods.

Tasked with keeping her prize upright, Belinda did not approach Audra, but she shouted a "Merry Christmas!"

Audra ran to Belinda and gave her a big squeeze around the waist. She whispered in her ear, "Merry Christmas" in return.

The two girls lived a fairy tale for a couple of weeks. The cabin made a great home base where Audra could hunt and Belinda could gather. Audra was always on the look-out for how it would end. She would search the woods for signs of other humans, for signs of zombies. They got zombies, but Audra would bait them into going the other direction. She would run away from them and then lose them. The zombies would continue until something else caught their eye.

But then one night Audra awoke to a crackling laughter in the pitch dark. She looked toward the entrance and saw that the whole front room was ablaze. The long flames shot this way and that, with the most heavily invested flames on the front door itself. The top half of the room's air was already filling with dark heavy smoke. Audra pushed on Belinda until she fell off the bed. Belinda groaned as her body hit the floor with a large thunk.

"Wake up, Belinda! Wake up!" Audra shouted.

Audra jumped over her sister and grabbed the rickety chair that neither of the girls was brave enough to use. She rammed the chair into the small glass window in the bedroom. Both the chair and the window broke. Audra used a leg of the chair to finish breaking out the glass. Belinda sat up but had pulled her legs close to her and wrapped her arms around them to create a small ball of a person.

"Belinda, you have to get up. Climb out this window. We have to go."

She could hear yelling outside. Audra pulled on Belinda, but she did not move. This was not the time to freeze. Audra slapped her hard in the face.

"GET UP NOW!"

Belinda, still in a daze, was at least now in a moving daze. She uncurled herself and Audra helped her crouched figure toward the window. She gave her a push and with some squeezing, Belinda was out the other side. Audra felt the heat invading the room. The mattress had gathered sparks and was about to catch. Audra grabbed her full pack, which she packed every night, and shoved it out the window. She followed behind it, landing on it before slinging it on. She grabbed whimpering Belinda by the arm and they ran.

"Is that them?" shouted a voice from the front of the cabin.

Audra grabbed Belinda's arm tighter and forced her at a speed that was not owned by Belinda. They kept tripping and falling all over the woods, smashing into trees, the scent of smoke still on their clothes. Belinda was sobbing, but Audra would not let her stop. Audra would never let her stop.

After the adrenaline had faded, fear still clung to their brains. They ran all night.

* * *

Dwyn arrived almost midday to the township, finding Audra passed out up against the border fence. He suspected there was a moonshiner not far from her current location. He threw a blanket on her, making his way to Vesna. An hour later, he returned to her body, which had not moved from its awkward position.

"Let me rest," she muttered, "I ran forty miles and beat your ass here."

Even hung-over, she still had a quick wit. Dwyn rolled his eyes before leaving her and returning to their last camping spot. Setting his things down, he pulled off his boots and climbed into the river. Dwyn took off one article at a time, scrubbing and wringing them out, leaving them on the bank to dry in the sun. Audra appeared unexpectedly. She sat on the bank and watched carefully, much to Dwyn's embarrassment and pleasure.

"Did you get in before the fire, last night?" asked Dwyn, standing deep in the water.

A pained look swept her face. Without a word, she stood up, grabbed his clothes and walked off. She dropped them several meters into the woods.

After a few days of errand running and zombie tagging, Audra and Dwyn were happy to bring the scientists their requested supplies. The gate was closed when the duo arrived. Audra was pleased to see that the place still looked abandoned. There were even a couple zombies surreptitiously tied up front to give the impression that the place was still overrun. Audra called out and Ryder emerged from the laboratory. She let out an excited squeal and gave them both a hug after she opened the gate. She barely allowed them to walk into the lab before she tore into the new supplies like a child on Christmas day. Audra was amazed to look around and see the lights on.

"Ryder got the solar panels working again," said a proud Satomi.

Ryder blushed.

"Well, Satomi has been managing this lab better than Lysent!" she said in a joke only the two of them seemed to understand.

The girls exchanged playful pushes until Ryder spotted a new device.

"Oh my! We've been dying without a centrifuge," Ryder said.

She forgot her modesty and jokes to rush a machine box over to the counter. Ziv tinkered with its settings, frowning at its features. Audra nodded and pretended she knew what a centrifuge was. She looked over the counters, covered in notebooks, beakers, and other science stuff. It looked like they had been busy.

"So, tell me more about what you're doing out here," said Audra.

Satomi smiled.

"So, as you know, the virus is only transferred by bodily fluids - typically from a bite. The virus shuts down the complex parts of the brain that make us who we are. The only things that run OK are the primal portions lower down, close to the spinal cord. That's the brain stem and the cerebellum."

"How does the virus know the difference?"

"It doesn't, actually. The virus only attacks a specific type of neurotransmitter whose primary role is communication in the more complex parts of the brain. The primal parts also use them, but not as extensively. Somehow the brain adapts to keep the primal parts functioning, but the rest of the brain cannot communicate. So the lungs keep breathing. The heart keeps beating. Gross motor function remains. The hunger response is there, too. The virus evolved to stimulate hunger in the presence of potential hosts so it could continue to replicate."

Satomi's answers made sense to Audra, so she dared to ask another question.

"Then, how do you cure it?"

"We introduce antiviral molecules with special tags into the bloodstream. Instead of attaching to the neurotransmitters, the virus attaches to them. This neutralizes them and then the body removes them through natural processes. The neurotransmitters slowly replenish and wake up the rest of the brain."

"Wow. How fast can you develop the antiviral?"

"Well, it will be slow if we have to develop it ourselves. We can do it. We're working on it. Replication would be much easier."

"So, if you had a sample of the cure, you'd have a head start?"

"A big head start."

Audra pondered over that for a moment. She couldn't help with all the science, but maybe she could help in other ways. The sooner they developed the cure, the better.

"Ryder, did you ever see where they keep the antidote?"

Ryder paused before answering.

"You want to steal us some?"

"Can it be done?"

Ryder thought about it.

"No, you always get escorted around, right? You'll never be able to get back to the secured area."

"Any time they are not in the secured area?" Audra prodded.

"No… well, I guess for transport to another township. The other townships hold their own infected and they like to keep it available for outbreaks."

There was only one way Lysent transported items from town to town. They were so damn proud of it.

"Do they use the train?"

"Yeah, they do," said Ryder seeing where Audra was going with this.

The antidotes would be most vulnerable en route on the train through the forest. If they could get a few samples, then they would be that much closer to replicating the cure. And Audra thought, even if it did not work out, she could steal one for Belinda. Perhaps this group was worth something after all.

"Train heist!" yelled out Dwyn.

Ziv contributed nothing to the conversation. He shook his head in disapproval. Everyone avoided asking for his opinion.

CHAPTER NINE

"I'm just so tired of it all," reported Belinda. "I'm tired of surviving, tired of death, tired of life."

"We have to keep going, Belinda. We have to take care of each other."

"Why?"

The question stung. Audra tried not to take it personally, but Belinda questioning both of their lives hurt. Belinda sat on the forest floor next to her first zombie kill. Her anger which had brought on the violence had turned to sadness. She had swung one way and was now the other. Audra imagined the statement pained her because of the truth within it. Belinda did look tired… of everything. Audra pulled a rag from her pocket and knelt down next to Belinda. She cleaned the splatter from her face. Belinda did not respond. She stared down at the blood-soaked animal corpse and the remains of the pups.

"They were my friends," said Belinda.

"I'm so sorry."

Audra was sorry, but there was no way they could have fed

themselves, a mama dog, and her litter of pups. Audra wondered how much Belinda had eaten in the past few days. A lot of the meat had gone to the dogs.

"I don't know why we keep doing this."

"Well, what do you want to do?"

Silence. Her eyes unwavering from the masses on the ground.

"If we weren't worried about surviving each day, what would you like to do?"

Belinda thought for a few moments. Audra herself had a difficult time conjuring a dream without an invading zombie.

"What would you like to see?" She prodded again.

Belinda's streams of tears faded as she spoke.

"Well, remember when we went on vacation and saw that waterfall?"

"Yes, I do. Mom and Dad made us walk up all those steps, but it was beautiful."

Belinda paused at the mention of their parents. Audra thought of the purple scarf their mom had worn that day. The wind kept sweeping it off her head. She remembered their dad walking up the steps behind her, pulling on the scarf to add to the trouble.

"I'd like to go there again," Belinda offered.

"Deal," said Audra without hesitation.

"What do you mean?"

"I mean, let's go. We're wandering anyway. Might as well go some place pretty, right? Let's go."

Belinda wiped her face with her sleeves. She gave the bloody dog one last look.

* * *

Ziv stood with the dissenters outside the plaza. His sign displayed disapproval of the corporate policy of waking the dead. The chants were easy to learn.

"Less dead means less food!"

"Keep them dead!"

In reality, he was watching Lysent move goods to the train depot to see if any antidotes were being transported today. Last week, it was nothing but food stores. Today, a small cart with a cooler on top, made its way from the laboratory to the convoy heading to the train station. Ziv cheered one more protest with the group then dismissed himself to signal Satomi. Audra noticed that he'd chosen the role farthest from the train. He didn't want to be associated with the theft. His survival instincts were strong.

For as fancy as the train technology was, the station was not - a loading dock and a passenger area. Several people mingled around, including cool and collected Satomi. As she walked by, she marked one of the round corners of a silver car with charcoal, the car which had a cooler from Lysent Laboratories in it. She hoped the scribble would stay for the swift train ride. Lysent cleared the railway of non-passengers and the rail buzzed to life. The train took off fast, too fast to jump on or off.

The train sped along until its computers alerted for an emergency stop. A fallen tree had smashed through both fences and lay on the rail. The buzzing noise of the lines faded as power was cut until the debris could be cleared. A young girl hiding in the brush watched the front car for a crew member to step out and investigate. It was not unusual for the trains to be unmanned. Seeing no one, she ran down the rail along the train, looking for the small charcoal mark. She had to hurry. Workers would be out soon. They weren't far from a station; the location of dying pines dictated their unfortunate proximity.

Audra then saw the mark. She rubbed it off the sleek metal with her sleeve before she slipped into the car. The shiny metal of the cooler was easy to spot among the wooden crates. She separated it from the others and examined it. It did not have a lock, but the black case surrounded by ice within it did. Audra did not dare take the whole container. GPS units were plentiful in the Lysent company. Plus, she hoped by only taking one vial that the theft might not be pinpointed to the train and the pine tree. Perhaps Lysent would think the antidote was stolen when packed or received. Audra listened outside for the crew to arrive or for the passengers to grow restless. She heard nothing. They still would have to remove the tree - she had time.

Audra set the black box on top of the closed cooler and pulled out a small metal tool set to pick the lock. It only took a moment to realize it was a hybrid, part mechanical and part electronic. She fished the electronic lighter provided by Vesna from her pocket. Did she have time? She pulled out its battery and some of the wires, stripped them with her knife and stuck them into the lock. The lock blew out when it made contact. She picked the mechanical part and opened the lid. There in insulation were thirty small vials labeled "Zombie Anti-Viral". She grabbed two, sticking one in each pocket. She closed the lid. The mechanical portion of the lock clicked, but Audra was sure the electronics were fried. She put it back into the cooler and pushed it back where she'd found it.

Audra glanced out of the car. She heard voices, but no one

was in view. A crew worked on the tree in the front, talking to each other about how unlucky it was that it had fallen on the tracks instead of any other way. She slipped down and underneath the train. It was a stupid place to be. At any point, they could clear the debris and turn the rail back on, electrocuting her. She crawled six cars down. Emerging from underneath, she walked down the track for a bit, hidden by the train. She could hear them chopping at the tree. When she had gotten some distance, she got off the track and found where the fence had been snipped in a few places for her to peel up and slide through. Dwyn had suggested she climb over, but the concertina wire at the top was not something Audra wanted to fight.

"Hey!" yelled a worker who happened to be by the fence, supervising the tree work.

Audra's face swung toward the voice out of reflex before she slipped through. The fence edges scratched her escaping body. Would they recognize the tree as sabotage? Maybe she was just an opportunistic thief scouting the train.

"It has come to my attention that someone has stolen antidote vials off the transport train. This is NOT how we do things. We cannot just wake up people without due process. As punishment, there will be no awakenings for the next six months. If you think things work better in *your* hands, we will keep *ours* off," Greenly announced to the crowd.

Audra hung back and listened. She heard the cries and frustration. Another half a year without their loved ones. Her job would be impacted, too. Negotiations would be different. If she found someone tomorrow, the family may decline to make a deposit. Why pay six months' rent? They might need that cash during the unpredictable winter. Tag them and come back later when it was more convenient to all parties involved, minus the tagger.

Audra herself would struggle to pay rent for another six months with low wages. Her only out was the second antidote.

Audra had considered keeping the second antidote secret. She questioned Satomi, who explained the antidote was unstable and sensitive to temperature changes. Audra did not want to risk ruining the dose. She needed the scientists' help. She disclosed her theft of two vials.

"No, our foremost concern is getting the antidotes out of Lysent's village and to the laboratory," Vesna stated, matching the determination in Audra's eyes.

Audra had ventured to ask Vesna for help to retrieve her sister. She feared the six-month probation. Lysent had quickly tied the antidote thefts to those interested in waking up loved ones. They had effective hostages under their roof and it would be easy for them to retaliate further. She needed to get Belinda out and they would not hand her over willingly.

Vesna packed the solar-powered cooler with the vials. The scientists were ecstatic to have real samples. Once they could replicate it, they could begin experiments on delivery systems. Audra had been told about Vesna's plan and knew the risks. They did not want to just wake up a bunch of people and hope those people would be on their side.

They would wake up everyone.

A large population increase would overwhelm the corporate systems and cause them to fail. It would destroy the economy as it stood. Then, the people would be forced to rely on themselves, on their own systems. And the corporation would lose their power. If Lysent wanted to limit the resources and population artificially, Vesna's group would do the opposite. They would aerosolize the cure, treating zombies at a distance en masse.

Audra had her doubts. A lot of the people enjoyed the corporation's care. Would they be able to rely on their own resources? Yes, the plan destroyed the corporation, but what was best for the current and future population? Audra stayed silent on the matter. She now had access to cure vials. Anything more than that, she did not care.

"Then Dwyn can escort the scientists back to the lab with the antidotes and I'll stay here and get my sister by myself. I think I have done more than my part, already."

Dwyn shot her a look that declared he did not like that idea at all. Audra knew he was determined to accompany her into Lysent.

"Vesna, Audra is a part of your group now - do you at least see her concerns?" asked Dwyn.

"I do, but having her sister roaming around my store and Lysent chasing after her isn't going to help our replication process!"

The outburst relayed to Audra that Vesna would not see it her way. Audra sighed.

"OK, let me run the antidotes by myself. I'll get them there in record time. Then will I have permission to come back here and figure out my sister?"

Vesna sighed and closed her eyes to think. Something had to give.

"You can run one antidote. Dwyn will take the other and the scientists behind you. When you both come back, we can TALK about what to do with your sister. Your sister's life isn't the only one at stake here."

Audra left in a huff. She would grab a few drinks while the crew got the antidotes ready for transport. At least she had control of that, despite what Dwyn and Vesna thought.

Audra returned a little less argumentative. She examined the new addition to her pack that Ryder had built. It was a small engineered cooler that used refrigerant from an old appliance and a small solar panel that attached to the top of Audra's pack. Dwyn thought it was the coolest thing. Ziv suggested that she run in sunny areas. Audra winced at the idea. The sun was rough on her fair skin, and being out in the open was less than ideal. He showed her how to read the efficiency of the small panel and the meter of the battery. She would only have to change course if the battery got too low. Audra hoped for a few well-timed sunny hours that would keep the battery full. Barring battery issues, it would only take a day and a half to get to the lab.

Audra set out on her run. Her head felt warm with her buzz. Only three miles in and the only thing she could think about was the antidote nestled in her bag. She could break out her sister and cure her. She had never had an opportunity like this. And now it was within her grasp. The scientists did not even have a plan for her sister. They wanted to wake up everyone that was roaming free, not just the ones with known loved ones on the other side. To appease her, they suggested the stored infected would be released when the corporation became disorganized and when villagers took over, but they did not know for sure. They did not know that at all. All the zoms in Lysent's possession could be destroyed as punishment. Enacting the six-month probation was a demonstration of that power.

Lysent's plaza and her sister were in the other direction, but she was now far enough away that she could turn around and sidestep the township which contained Vesna and the others. Audra would wake up her sister and they would run off together. Dwyn would understand. They had the backup sample, anyway. She had trained Dwyn well. He would provide the backup and make sure that the group's efforts were not in vain. She would not be hurting anyone, just slowing them down for a few days while they waited for Audra's return. It was their fault, anyway. Why would they entrust Audra with the antidote when she was the only one with a sick loved one? Or, was she? Did the others have loved ones they cared about in waiting? Audra had never thought to ask. Their common goal was the dismantling of the corporation. Audra had not looked further than that.

No, it didn't matter. She did not care if Lysent stood or fell, if the scientists had people they cared for or not, she needed to make things right.

Audra turned around and went southwest. She would run far around the township and then make a beeline to the corporation. Audra would have plenty of time to consider a plan. She had hoped breaking out her sister would be a two-person job, but she couldn't trust Dwyn to understand her subterfuge. He would try to change her mind. Her duty was to her sister, not to him or any others.

Her footsteps matched her heartbeat in both cadence and determination. Each was a march, not just a step away from the laboratory and all it meant, but a step forward to her sister.

CHAPTER TEN

The mugginess of the morning amplified the sun's heat and made Audra stir. Without opening her eyes, she could tell she was alone in the tent. Belinda's presence was a strong force. You always knew when she was near.

With Belinda starting a fire and gathering breakfast, Audra rested her aching bones in the still quiet. Quiet was something missing from Audra's life, even in the woods when most of the population had been rendered speechless. Audra spent most of her days comforting and loving on her sister, encouraging her, and listening to her problems. She had to be there for her, and the sun-speckled morning before Belinda woke was sometimes the only peaceful moment Audra experienced during the day. Audra decided to laze for a few moments more.

They were seven days into their journey. In just a few more, Audra expected to hear the sound of rushing water. They could camp near the bridge closest to the edge. Audra wished the falls would conjure to life something in Belinda she had not seen in a while - hope.

As the warmth filtered onto her face, a shuffling threatened to upend her peace. Soon it was closer. A figure leaned up against the tent, clawing haphazardly at the canvas, trying to get inside. Audra sighed. So much for a quiet morning. Belinda must be out gathering wood or water, for she had not screamed out. A zom was out there, threatening to damage their hard-won tent. Audra slipped on a long shirt and hat and pulled out her dagger. With the zom still focused on one of the side walls, Audra unzipped the front of the tent and stepped out.

The zom was much taller than her, but with a quick jump, she sliced into his softened temple. His curly red hair tinged with darkness as he crumpled onto the tent, much to Audra's dismay. She pushed him off. She knew she should drag his stench away from the campsite, but it was just so early in the morning. They would leave soon, anyway. She compromised by pulling him behind the tent and let him be, with his arms above his head and his legs dragged straight. While this was not how she had wanted to start her morning, she imagined this was not how he had wanted to spend his, either.

The humidity found in the tent was not present outside, and the warmth gave way to the still chilly morning. Knowing Belinda would have veered off if she spotted the zombie, Audra readied herself to go seek her out. Entering the tent to add another layer of clothes, she noticed Belinda's pack, neatly disassembled as if she was taking inventory. Audra wondered why she had not woken up for that activity. She glanced over the items. Belinda had left anything needed to carry water, and her usual bundling material to gather sticks also remained inside the tent. Where had Belinda gone? Audra pushed back the disturbed feeling settling in her heart as she stepped out to decipher her sister's last movements in the campsite.

She did not have to look far to find the note sitting by the remains of last night's fire. The little bird statue Audra had received at Christmas weighed down the small paper. At once, her mother's voice sprung forward and echoed in her head.

"Take care of your sister. You are all she has left."

Audra rushed in the direction of the falls without even thinking to grab her own pack. She ran, realizing that all she had left was her sister.

* * *

Audra ran, lost in the nuances of stealing a person from a corporation's prison. Thoughts in stationary positions seemed just that, stationary. With motion, she encouraged and pushed her thoughts forward. Each step gave a new view, a new perspective, both physically and mentally. Audra focused on the problem at hand as she worked through the brush. The leaves crunched underneath her. She stayed off the path. She wanted no one to know where she was going and at what time.

Audra needed supplies - something to cut the clear acrylic that kept her from her sister, a suction cup to pull the plastic toward her so she could lower it to the ground, and perhaps a firearm to make their escape. Could she fight her way out? Would she?

She could inject her sister through one of the air holes. How long would the wake-up process take? Besides the bite on her forearm, she was a perfect specimen. Would Belinda be able to recognize her after the injection? Would she be able to help in her escape? Audra realized that Lysent had kept the whole process hidden for a reason. It was doubtful that the antidote was fast-acting. But what if she took the escape out of the equation? She could administer the cure using the air holes near the floor. Belinda would wake up, eventually.

Lysent would know who stole their antidote, but she would be long gone. She would never show her face in the townships again. She would lose Belinda. Belinda would curse her name, saying she abandoned her, but she would be safe and healthy. She would find friends and a life in the township. And as much as Audra longed to see her smile of recognition, she also knew it would be OK to just make things right.

It was settled. She would visit Belinda, give her the antidote, and then run far from here.

Audra ran past the township where Vesna and the others waited for word that the cure had made it to the laboratory. Instead, she arrived on the outskirts of the township housing Lysent and her beloved Belinda. She slowed to a walk to gather herself and automatically pulled out a snack. If it all worked out, she would soon run again, faster than ever for a long time. Audra considered camping and resting for the night. Rest could do good before Lysent's goons were on her tail. But, a glance at the battery meter shaded her with doubt, and the scientists would grow nervous concerning Audra's absence. No, she would have to summon the strength to save herself when the time came.

With the corporation in her sights, it was time to prepare. What would she need for her long journey into the wilderness? How light would she need to keep her pack to outrun Lysent's horses? How long would they chase her? What else was out there? Audra didn't know, and she didn't care. She only hoped they would release her sister when she rose.

Audra set aside the solar panel. An indentured tagger would not have such high technology and gear. Her fingers gently pulled the antidote out of the cooler. As she knelt to hide the panel and cooler in the brush, she heard a crunch, crunch,

crunch.

THUMP!

With a well-placed tackle, Audra found herself on her side on the ground. It was not long before she found out who was on top of her.

"WHAT THE HELL ARE YOU DOING, AUDRA?!" yelled out Dwyn, his face in hers.

Despite his anger and her surprise, her body involuntarily responded to his warm frame on top of hers. The reaction confused her, and she did not respond. Dwyn also looked uncomfortable. He pulled off of her but did not help her up.

"You're taking the antidote to your sister, aren't you?" he said in a calmer voice.

Audra stayed silent, sitting on her rear. She pulled her knees close and brushed leaves off of her pants and arms. She couldn't be angry about the tackle. She had deceived him. Dwyn paced in front of her, panting from the chase and jump. He was also covered in debris, but that did not concern him.

"That isn't yours. You're stealing it," he tried to explain.

Audra bit her tongue. It was not his either. And she had already stolen it once. But she understood.

He crouched down close to her.

"Audra, I thought we were… friends. Why would you go behind my back?"

She looked down at the ground between her knees. She could not look at him. Audra could convince herself that she couldn't care less about the scientists, but Dwyn was another story. Dwyn's trust and camaraderie meant something to her. She wasn't sure what though. Sometimes it reminded her of her sister, but she dared to consider in a more complete or equal way. There was more give and take. And, she had just dared to take a lot.

"I had to, Dwyn, I'm sorry. I owe it to my sister. This is my best bet to make it right."

He grabbed her by the arms and gently shook until she met his gaze. He did not understand.

"Make *what* right?"

The gravity of leaving everything behind and embarking into the western wilderness away from not just Lysent, but Dwyn and Belinda, sank in. Her face did not change shape, but still, tears came steady, tracing the edges of her cheekbones and falling onto her collar.

A simple and convicted, "It's my fault," fell from her mouth.

It answered no questions, but he motioned to bring her closer and she fell into him, knocking him off balance and sending the pair backward. Pinning him underneath her, Audra cried until there were no more tears, which took much longer than either expected.

When the tears stopped, Audra found herself still buried in Dwyn's chest. He was warm and heavy. Audra rolled off of him and onto the ground next to him. They lay side by side with no words. Dwyn did not push her to explain. He was content for a moment to know Audra did not take pleasure in abandoning him or the others. They stared into the tree branches and the sky in between the leaves until Audra found her voice. She was surprised how composed and calm it was.

"It's my fault Belinda was bitten. I'm the only one looking out for her now. Sending the world into chaos by waking up everyone outside does not help her chances. She's inside."

"OK."

"OK? Okay - what?"

"We will get your sister out before we release the antidote.

I'll convince Vesna. But let us work on the replication first, so we're ready. You can have the second dose if we accidentally destroy the first. You risked the most to get them. It should be your payment.

"You've waited three years. Can you wait another couple of months?"

Audra attempted to wipe her face, but she felt the wetness smear. She pushed it around as her thoughts cleared. Waiting on people and being part of a group was not her specialty. She would rather depend on herself and get things done. This required trust and patience. But, it also afforded an alternative to waking up her sister and disappearing off the face of the earth. In a perfect world, she could wake up her sister right before Lysent came tumbling down. Then things would be made right on all levels, and they would be together.

"Give us a chance, Audra. Don't run from us."

He sent his request into the sky but did not want to miss her response. He rolled onto his side, his elbow on the ground and his face on his hand. Dwyn took his flannel sleeve and wiped at her face. There was no helping it though.

Maybe she would give this a try if just for a while.

"I shouldn't have run…" she admitted.

Dwyn said nothing, but continued to touch her face with the cuff of his sleeve, then moved to his hand. Her skin felt cool with the tears evaporating from the surface. His hand felt rough and strong. Audra closed her eyes to the touch and was jolted ever so slightly when she felt his lips touch hers. She leaned forward and felt his hand in her hair. He guided her back down with a hand at her hip.

CHAPTER ELEVEN

"It is good you are here this time," said Satomi in her genuine way.

It was not meant as a jab, but it reminded Audra that she had been missing during the last two human trials to replicate the antidote. While she had consigned herself as part of the group now, she still felt out of her element in the confines of the laboratory. She spent days, near weeks, at a time occupying herself by tagging in the woods as the scientists worked.

Vesna had not been surprised when Dwyn told her of Audra's transgression. There was a reason Audra had only been given one vial. Vesna had expected Audra would act out of dire need, but hoped she would also figure out she needed the group, and the group needed her. Vesna stated she would not tell the others of Audra's excursion. They could all work together a while longer, even if their goals were different.

The first two attempts to replicate the antiviral had failed and killed its subjects. Ryder understood there would be failures before success, and tolerated the deaths. Satomi, more in the medical field where it was "first do no harm," had the most trouble accepting that harm was inevitable. After many weeks, the group was ready to test their new version of the reproduced antidote.

Satomi, Ryder, and Ziv hung back as Audra and Dwyn looked in the front window of the building that served as their miniature corral. It was rumored among the taggers that Lysent regularly rounded up the unwanted zoms with yellow tags. Lysent kept high-traffic areas like the townships and the railway clear, by creating large outdoor corrals to keep the sick out of sight. But unlike a Lysent corral, Ziv knew many of the people in his place of work. Satomi pleaded with him not to share any information, but just let them pick one at random. It felt unethical to make an informed choice on whom to wake up. It felt even more unethical this early in the trials when it was more likely to kill the subject than cure her.

"We've just been opening the door and letting one slip out," said Satomi.

"Well, that's not going to work this time," Audra replied.

Zombies swarmed the front door and window, drawn by the previous activity. Scientists peeking into the windows during the day had not helped either. The windows needed to be covered before the zombies tore each other apart. Audra sent Dwyn for a window cover as she circled the building. The next window showed a separate room, closed off, and empty. They would use Satomi's strategy, but with another door. Audra finagled the lock on the window and slipped inside. The room seemed to serve as a second office and storage area; a desk sat in the center, but cleaning and extra office supplies also shared the space. Audra hid behind the interior door to the zoms as she opened it halfway. She resisted the urge to show her face to the zoms and instead allowed Ryder and Satomi to relay the information to her.

"Three maybe," shouted Ryder.

"Oh, there are more!" called out Satomi.

She was not surprised to hear others were coming. They may not have seen the door, but they saw their comrades change directions and followed their lead. Just as Audra was growing impatient, one cleared the doorway. It met Audra's boot at once then hit the floor. She shut the door on the others.

The door did not close but bounced off more flesh.

A forearm poked through.

The floored zombie spiked with energy, feeding off the smell of life coexisting in the room. It both tried to pivot on the ground to eye its prey and stand up to charge, resulting in a half-crouched spin. Audra still had a few moments while it gained control of its stubborn body. She returned her focus to the door through which it had come. Audra held pressure on it with her body as she tried to return the arm to its owner on the other side. She had to avoid its claw while being careful not to slip her arm into its face.

She had gotten all but the hand through when she noticed added pressure on the door. A third zombie had arrived and was adding its weight. Audra gave a glance at the first zombie, who had settled on crawling toward her feet. She could ask for help. Dwyn would come help. But it seemed silly to ask for help for one on the floor and two against the door. That was child's play. But to Audra's surprise, it was not Dwyn that pulled himself through the window. With Audra's smiles of encouragement, Satomi walked behind the infected on the floor and gingerly pulled it away by its ankles. Her job completed, she moved as far away as possible from it, while Audra untangled the doorway of limbs and confirmed the firm click of the door mechanism.

Their subject was a male, mid-thirties when he turned. His face was strong and angular, his glasses skewed but not broken on his face. He was lucky to have them still. There were few places to get prescription lenses currently. No one was making them as far as Audra knew, only collecting them. The township had a glasses library. You would try on pairs until you found one that improved your vision, but it was better to have just kept up with yours.

His hair had continued to grow in his state, but it was apparent it was previously short and neat, even gelled conservatively. It was easy to see he was a strong fellow despite the recent atrophy of his muscles. He had found his feet and was doing a Frankenstein's monster walk toward them in his mussed lab coat.

Ryder stuck her head through the window to see their progress.

"Oh, he is big! I wonder if the antidote is mass dependent..." she said as she dropped back out to discuss the scenario with Ziv.

Audra pinched the bridge of her nose and squeezed her eyes shut to summon patience from the front of her face. Even without a degree in science and having grown up basically in the wild, it still sounded like something they should have figured out before asking her to retrieve someone. She realized she might have created a mass-dependent problem of her own. The exit window was small. Satomi, who had sneaked behind Audra for safety, appeared to be thinking the same thing.

"Erm, maybe we should tie the subject up before we attempt this window."

Audra nodded in agreement and Satomi poked her head

outside to ask Ziv for some rope.

A small smile drew on Audra's lips as she realized she had come into the building to wrangle a zombie, not even bothering to bring a rope. She was becoming overconfident, cocky even. Ziv's small hand gripping rope appeared in the room through the window.

For a sheltered scientist, Satomi seemed willing to help out when it came to the infected. Audra saw her approach was respectful, almost religious, like a person preparing someone for sacrifice. Audra pinned the zom's arms against his body. With the rope in hand, Satomi pulled his wrists together.

"Actually, nobody likes bondage scars. Let's do this instead," said Audra.

She directed the rope around his chest, wrapping his arms tight on each side. Satomi nodded and assisted.

"But for the record, there is, or at least was, a select demographic that like bondage scars."

Satomi's dry chide surprised Audra. She burst out in laughter as she looked at their scientific zombie. It was possible.

With the arms under control, Satomi managed the upper half of their standing zombie while Audra wrapped the rope around his legs. She tied it off with a surgeon's knot before she and Satomi switched places. With a warning to Ziv and the others outside the window, Satomi picked up the zombie's legs as Audra knocked him off balance. They headed with their cargo to the window. By this point, Audra ordinarily would have named the zombie, but this one was different. He would have a name soon. Or not. The thought weighed on Audra more than the body did.

They pushed him through the window until he reached a tipping point. He tilted at an angle and slid. They heard a thump and a crunch as the side of his face hit the ground.

His glasses.

"We'll just tell him that they were broken when we met him," Audra whispered to Satomi with a half smile.

Audra could tell that Satomi enjoyed being included on the secret. With the man's legs still in the window, Audra squeezed out. She pulled him away so Satomi could exit as ungracefully as needed. Her slim body slipped through with no problem, impressing Audra.

Dwyn pulled the zombie up on its bound feet. Audra pulled off the ropes from his legs. He was too heavy to carry around. She tied the rope around his waist as a leash of sorts. He liked her and it took little persuading to have him follow her toward the laboratory. Audra wondered if she should salvage his glasses. One lens was still intact, but he did not look willing to allow Audra to reach for them. Audra did not know if zoms needed vision correction. She left them on, just in case.

The odd procession made its way between two counters. Satomi had shown glimmers of lightheartedness, but back in the lab with her colleagues, it seemed responsibility lay heavy on her again. Audra could not decide if it was because she respected life, or because maybe she doubted their formula. Ziv barely entered the room. He leaned against the wall, looking rather bored. Audra's side glance accused him of wanting to be closest to the exit, but Ziv did not move closer.

The zombie seemed overstimulated with the surrounding crew, anyway. He gained energy and pulled at his restraints. He turned to Dwyn and teetered dangerously on his feet. Audra, who stood in front of him, gave a giant clap to bring his attention back to her. No one made mention he looked like he was fighting what was to come. Ryder's hand shook ever so gently as she readied the serum and handed it to Satomi, who approached the subject from behind.

"Subject Three, thank you for your service. It will change the world," she said with a whisper.

And with that, she leaned over with a syringe and injected him in the shoulder. Subject Three turned his head toward the stimulus. Dwyn used two hands to grab the sides of Subject Three's face with a firm grip to keep Satomi safe. She did not flinch as she finished injecting the serum. Ryder requested that Subject Three be escorted to the observation room. It was almost anticlimactic, Audra thought. She expected some immediate reaction, like convulsions or at least a yawn of the jaw. Instead, they left Subject Three in the small conference room, no different than before.

"I'll take first watch," offered Satomi.

"I'll stay, too," added the curious Audra.

Ryder fidgeted and then left to clean up the laboratory. Dwyn helped. Ziv continued his work on aerosolizing formulas with similar molecular weight. There had been an argument as to whether this was the best way to go, but Vesna was set on aerosolizing the antidote and waking up masses.

Audra and Satomi observed Subject Three walk circles around the conference room, which was empty besides the table. Previously, they'd used it as a space to eat meals. They took out the chairs, but the table proved more difficult to remove.

There was no big reaction. Nothing at all yet. Audra was not sure if that was a good thing or a bad thing. She didn't want to offend by asking. Twenty minutes passed and Audra considered moving onto other things, when Satomi broke the silence.

"What is different about him?" she asked.

Her head gave a slight tilt, indicating a thought process

forming inside. Audra looked at Subject Three. He was still walking in circles around the table, like a slow hamster on a wheel. He maintained the same slouched posture as before. His mouth was slack-jawed. Underneath his broken glasses, his eyes looked dead, blinking. Blinking. Audra watched his eyes. He blinked again.

"He is blinking," her tone pitched upwards, her excitement growing.

"Blinking is a parasympathetic response. Infected humans blink," Satomi dismissed.

"Yes, but not this often. This is… human often."

Satomi followed.

"It is unusual. Definitely a change in his behavior. Maybe his nociceptive neurons are firing."

Audra wasn't sure what that meant, but she had been observing zombies for years. She spotted them passing through terrain as she hid in fields or above in the trees. They all had a certain range of motion and behavior. There was something different about the one in their conference room. Someone was inside, stuck inside that sick body. Audra's thoughts turned to her sister. Belinda was in there, imprisoned in her body, in her cell, in that wretched corporation. And Audra had put her there. It was her fault. All of it.

That thought in the back of her head came slowly burning to the front. She needed out, away from others, away from herself. Without another word to Satomi or mention of the developments to the others, Audra walked out. Satomi could tell the others. Even if the process was successful, it would be slow. He was just blinking now. If it was unsuccessful, it would be slower. She had time. Without knowing where she was going, Audra walked from the laboratory door to the entrance of the small plaza. She let herself through the gate. Her knees and feet picked up higher as she found speed. She did not bother to tell herself it was a scout run, a supply run, or a perimeter check. It was not any of those things. She was running because she needed to run.

Audra kept all her senses open and alert, but the meditative motion of her cycling legs left her mind churning. She did not find relief. Her emotions bubbled up, unknown sudden emotions not safely tied to specific thoughts. As she wondered if she would burst, the feelings would subside as if she had made distance from them by running faster than they could keep up. Then a new surge of feelings. It came like waves, rolling in and out. Audra did not cling to anything for fear it would consume her. It was not safe to run like this, but it seemed even less safe to be alone, stagnant, and sitting in her thoughts.

From behind a tree, someone walked across her path. Audra almost collided into her. She skidded to a stop and only years of suppressing instinct prevented her yelp of surprise. But it didn't stop her trembling or falling backward. The infected woman turned to look at her, her blond hair stuck to the sides of her face, her blue eyes huge and hungry. Young, alone, and lost, she reached her arms out and Audra thought for a moment to reach back. The vicious, teeth-filled snarl forced Audra to roll off to the side, tears in her eyes. Emotions she could not handle or name flooded her, her vision, her discernment, and what felt like her identity.

Just run.

It came to the forefront of her mind. Audra could almost see the words in her vision, blurring the zombie approaching her. She picked herself off the damp, leaf-littered ground and obeyed. Audra would run away, just like she had run away all those other times. Just like she had run away by throwing her sister into that corporation.

She had not done enough. Her sister had been trapped for years while she was out here. Why did she deserve to survive over her sister? What made her so special? Her anger pushed her legs to work harder and her chest expanded to keep up. Her arms did not flail in grief or fear but pumped, propelling her forward. She felt that fleeting pleasure of sprinting before her legs slowed. She stayed on that brink, back and forth between fast running and sprints.

She came upon a grassy field mowed short by animals. Audra made it halfway across when she flung herself onto the warm ground. She gasped for air. Her body was exhausted. For a moment, she focused on that. She focused on her breath, her expanding rib cage, the dizziness in her head. It grounded her. Putting her body in that catastrophic state allowed it to sync with her mind. Then placing that writhing body on the firm earth, she hoped to ground the abstract things behind her eyes.

If she could just identify what she was feeling, perhaps she could handle it. Why did she freak out over blasted blinking? Those first signs of life made her feel angry and resentful. Was she angry the virus had taken so much from her, or was she angry that she was about to get some of those things back? Though she was already flat-backed on the ground, that thought knocked her over.

She loved her sister. Her sister deserved life. But Audra had known this life and this purpose for so long. What was next for her? Audra avoided any more thoughts. It did not matter. Her obligation to her sister mattered. She had caught her breath. She pulled herself off the ground. The sun was making its journey to the other side of the earth. She needed to get back to the laboratory and face what was happening there. Audra sucked in her lips at the thought, took a deep breath, and brushed herself off. She was sweaty from her run, the grass and straw stuck to her body and dried, her face covered in dried tears she did not remember spilling. Despite the physical mess, she realized she could return to the laboratory. Countless times she had run straight to a moonshiner. She would get herself trashed and become incapacitated for hours. It provided relief, but here was some relief too. It was not as perfect and absolute as alcohol could achieve, but it had become bearable. Dwyn would be surprised at her same-day return.

Audra began her walk back. Her muscles stiffened from their strain and sudden stop. She worked them as she walked and soon they loosened. Everywhere the grass touched, her wet skin itched. Audra rubbed her hands along her arms until she found her way to the creek. She could follow it to familiar territory and the lab. Before moving on, she took off her clothes and boots and slipped into the cool water to rinse. She imagined all the emotions she had been carrying floating away as debris. It felt good to be clean. She climbed onto a small rock outcropping that was smooth and wonderfully warm from the sun. She lay there, eyes closed, finding peace.

Audra heard a rustle. Having spent years in the isolated wood, her instinct was no longer to cover up in modesty. It was all too often an animal or a nonjudgmental zombie. She felt safe on the outcropping. She looked to her right over the water to her clothes draped over rocks. There was movement in the woods. Audra squinted her eyes adjusting to the sun as the woman emerged.

It was the blond she had run into earlier in her run. Now in a calmer place, she considered tagging the zombie or at least securing it to increase the safety of the woods. No feeling was worse than finding yourself in a precarious situation with a zombie you dismissed earlier. The woman was drawn to the raw scent on the clothes, but could not find Audra. She wandered the bank, searching the ground. Her hair hung and covered her face. Audra could not stop watching. It felt like watching Belinda on those days when she looked lost in the world, confused over where she was and why. Those times, Audra would hold her hand in silence and hope she would come back to her.

Could the antiviral bring her back and then some? Audra imagined a Belinda more self-aware, confident, and steady. Her eyes returned to the lost zom. Either way, that could be home again.

The woman wandered away, having never found motion connected to the scent. Audra slid off the rock and waded to her clothes. She was going to go home. It was a long journey, not to the laboratory, but to finding her sister inside her sister. Belinda would be home. And if Belinda was home, Audra was home.

Audra walked on.

CHAPTER TWELVE

Audra returned to the laboratory and ignored Dwyn's surprised look. Both Satomi and Ziv were working. Ziv peered up from his work and eyed her wet hair.

"How is Subject Three?" she asked.

Ziv set down the pair of beakers and continued to stare her down.

"Where were you?"

"I had to deal with some things," she said, shrugging off her misadventure.

He squinted his eyes to analyze her answer.

"Did you tell someone what we were doing?"

"Stop," she said with tiredness in her voice rather than anger or defense, "I'm not a spy."

"Then why did Dwyn have to go get you when you were moving the antidote?"

"I ran into trouble. There is trouble out there if you didn't notice. Now, how is Subject Three?"

Satomi broke in.

"Ryder is watching him. He is continuing to exhibit aberrant behavior, atypical from the classic locomotive traits of those of his condition normalized for size."

Audra looked around for help.

"He rubbed his face," Dwyn offered.

Audra glanced around the room. No one had spoken up for her when Ziv accused her, but no one looked like they agreed either. She did not worry about him. He did not seem capable of much more than dissenting speeches and weaseling out of his chores. Before Audra decided whether to further address the topic, Ryder stuck her head into the main portion of the laboratory.

"You should come see," was all she said before her head disappeared again to watch her keep.

Everyone assumed *you* to be the plural 'you' and walked the paces to the observation area. Subject Three had slumped over the table, twitching and threatening to fall off. No one knew if this was part of the process or if he was dying.

"This might get worse," stated Audra.

She looked around for some bindings. Dwyn was right behind her, preparing to open the conference room door. Satomi stood guard as the two entered the room. They hoisted the man fully onto the table, his face sliding on the slick table. Audra and Dwyn log-rolled him supine. His jaw hung open but wagged at the sight of Audra. Then his eyes faded and the reaching of his chin lessened. Either his innate desire to eat humans had subsided or he was no longer aware of his surroundings. Audra tried to be gentle with the tired body, wrapping the long length of rope around his body, arms, and table, avoiding the spread-eagle look. He would be secure, safe, and accessible to the scientists.

Satomi took advantage of that access immediately. She examined with a comfortableness that Audra found refreshing if not worrisome. She tested his pupils with a flashlight, checking dilation and eye movement. She took his temperature from his armpit, avoiding his mouth, and left the room without giving voice to any of her thoughts.

Audra watched the patient on the table. She remembered the time her sister got sick and stayed in the hospital when hospitals were still big corporations, light switches worked, and her family existed. She remembered looking down at her sister, hoping the medicines worked so they could go play again. Now, she looked down at this guy, not knowing his life, and wished the same. She hoped the medicines worked, so she and her sister could go play again.

Her soak in the creek had refreshed her, but she had not replenished all her energy. A wave of tiredness washed over her as the adrenaline, emotions, and nervous energy dissipated. With the sun still up, she wanted a nap. She would need her rest to cover her shift later. Audra gave Dwyn a small touch on the shoulder to signal her upcoming disappearance. They both exited the conference room and Audra found her way to an office that served as her room for the nights she stayed in the industrial park.

The brightness from the windows showed the contents of the converted office. There were papers and books shoved in the corner, the remnants of the previous tenant. She would have left them where they were, but they were stacked precariously on all the horizontal surfaces. She did not want them to topple in her sleep or during a quick exit. To slip on a pool of loose paper was not her idea of an efficient escape plan. Messes like these were rare. No one had this amount of stuff anymore.

She dry-brushed her teeth before fluffing the blankets and soft things she had collected. She considered pulling another blanket from her pack, but that would be a blanket she would not have if vultures forced her out. Sleeping inside was still difficult despite having done it for the last week. The ceiling seemed so far away as compared to her tent. She lay her head underneath the desk for some protection. From what, she did not appreciate. She slipped into a fitful sleep.

Audra woke up to a dark room. Was it time for her shift? She hoped no one had peeked to find her tucked under the desk. She wandered out into the main area. No one was out and about. The silence was heavy. Perhaps they had retired to their rooms. But as she reached the observation area, she discovered the entire crew, having pulled all manners of seats together to watch.

"We considered waking you, but there isn't much to see," whispered Dwyn.

Despite his claim, his eyes did not veer from the subject. The others barely acknowledged her. Audra looked through the window frame and understood. Inside was not quite human and not quite zombie.

"Did he untie himself?"

"He did."

Zombies did not have the fine motor skills to untie knots or even the problem-solving skills to realize they were tied up. They gave constant force to whatever was in their way. Some things moved, and some things did not. But, despite Subject Three's ability to untie himself, he still did not seem aware of his surroundings. He did not examine the door or attempt escape; however, Audra noticed a chair was propped underneath the doorknob on their side as a new fortification. The subject shuffled around and around the conference table. He directed his eyes downward, which was not uncommon for zombie or human alike, but he also occasionally brushed his left hand on his shirt, as if he was pressing out wrinkles. A nervous habit from his previous life, for sure.

"Have you made any attempts to communicate?" Audra asked.

"Not yet," said Satomi. "He doesn't appear to be in any distress, so we don't want to stimulate him and activate any lower portions of his brain based on survival or hunger. We don't want to slow his progress."

"If he looks distressed, we'll try to talk to him," added Ryder.

Every time someone considered retiring for the evening, or even just spending time elsewhere in the laboratory, Subject Three would perform some new subtle task that would leave everyone talking about its meaning, his progression, and what they thought his next steps would be. Satomi believed functions would return in order of importance to survival based on the structure and hierarchy of the brain. Ziv based his theory on biochemistry. As the levels of neurotransmitters increased, the brain would wake up as a whole, but slowly. Ryder with no complete medical knowledge still thought a good theory was that he would be like a stroke victim, with damage and healing unique to the patient.

Then, Subject Three did what no zombie would do.

He sat down.

Zombies sat up, stood up, walked and ran all the time, but they did not sit down. It was an unforeseen milestone. They cheered and hugged. Subject Three was still in a mental fog, but he had the modern human tendency to sit when given the opportunity. Ziv offered everyone high-fives and went to work on creating the aerosol version for this antidote version. Even if the antidote formula needed tweaking, his work would not be completely off. He hurried away, excited and patting himself on the back for his part. Ryder disappeared and reappeared with a sheepish shrug and a bottle of champagne. She smiled and reported laboratories usually had a bottle hiding around for that special breakthrough.

"It's not time yet," she said with a sly smile, "but soon."

"Maybe he can drink it with us," said Satomi with honor and pride seeping through her words and into her smile.

They all nodded and Ryder slipped out of the room to tuck away the bottle until the proper time.

Dwyn and Satomi retired for the evening. Having just taken a nap, Audra was not ready for bed, and stayed up with the enthusiastic Ziv and dedicated Ryder. Audra tried to balance learning with not getting in the way. Ryder loved to teach and explain. She showed her how she was using cell cultures to create the antiviral proteins she desired. Audra had to stay a safe distance away to avoid contaminating the cultures under the sterile hood. It was easy to accidentally introduce bacteria that would kill or overwhelm the colony. It amazed Audra that these microscopic cells contained the answers to their big world problem.

Ziv huffed and grunted as he moved objects around his counter. Audra did not bother him. His efforts appeared to be more trial and error, so the process was not fun to explain. He was attempting to add air to protein solutions of similar weight as the antidote. Ryder explained there were a lot of big questions about the process. Could they aerosolize it without denaturing the protein? Would the method of inhalation work? What would be an effective dose? What was the ratio of dispersed versus delivered? Most would be lost to the environment, the patients' clothes, the ground, their face. Would it have to be inhaled or could it be absorbed through other mucous membranes - eyes, nose, tongue? Why did zombies have to breathe so shallowly? Ziv had a lot on his plate.

Audra didn't have to understand it all to realize it was a complicated undertaking. In the back of her mind, she considered a Plan B. If they provided a supply of antidotes to the villagers, the villagers would seek and demand their families. It would be a different structure of a rebellion and maybe safer for her sister. Audra said nothing for now. The scientists seemed hell bent on doing things for the greater good, not for individuals, not for themselves. They would take convincing.

Audra's mind and body were tired. She did not realize how long difficult days and nights could be. They were usually shortened by a strong concoction which let her mind swim in soporific numbness. Choosing to stay sober was not just one decision, but many. It was much easier to say 'yes' the first time than to say 'no' one million times. Tired of the process, Audra made motions she would try to sleep again. Ryder looked over her shoulder.

"You look wiped. It's been a long day for everyone. Have you eaten?"

Audra shook her head and wandered to their collective food store for something she might find appetizing. She did not know why she bothered. If you were not excited about food blocks or other dried food, you were long lost for something to strike your fancy. Audra chose a food block that appeared to have more oats than the protein substance Audra found chalky.

When the food bar was finished, Audra wished them both a good night. Ryder gave a small smile over her shoulder. Ziv made a *humph* noise that Audra assumed meant that he was upset she would go to bed when he was working on something important. But Audra could not help him with his important thing, so there was not much to do.

Subject Three was still sitting on the floor against the wall, slumped with his eyes closed. For a moment, her heart crept to her throat as she watched for breath. Was he dead? No, he appeared to be sleeping, another impossibility of the zoms that moved unceasingly. Audra wondered how much longer the process would take. Sleep healed, but she imagined that an awakening brain did not produce a dreamless sleep. He twitched, confirming Audra's thoughts. She wished him and herself a still night. Audra did not want her thoughts to devolve into dreams, but she already knew they would.

The next morning, she pulled herself out from under the desk and wiped the cold sweat from her brow. Last night's clothes hung over the wooden chair to freshen. It was not the same as rinsing them in the creek and letting them dry in the wooded sunshine, but at least they were spending time away from her body. Audra slipped them on over her base layer. She always left some semblance of clothes on, just in case. Most of her life was about just in case, because many times, it was the case.

As she slipped into the hall, sleepiness muffled her hearing, but she recognized conversations in the laboratory. One voice was strange. Without another moment passing, she was awake, alert, and her knife had made its way from her waist to her hand. She crept down the hall searching for signs of distress. The voices sounded neither happy nor strained. Audra stood just on the other side of the doorway, out of sight and listened.

It was Subject Three.

It must be Subject Three.

They were questioning him. And he was answering them.

Audra stepped into the doorway and saw that the conference room converted into an observation room for Subject Three had now become a conference room once more. Subject Three sat upright in a hard-backed chair. He almost looked to be interviewing for a job, except one lens of his glasses was broken, which was not acceptable interview attire. The man looked pale and nervous, but otherwise trying to give a good impression. He shifted nervously in his chair, and Audra wondered if they had offered him necessities such as the bathroom, food, and water, prior to his inquisition.

Dwyn stood up from his seat and smiled at Audra.

"Audra. Meet Gordon. He was a scientist here before the infection. Gordon, this is Audra. She is a warrior."

Audra's eyes narrowed a bit at this description of her occupation. It brought up images of warring people attacking each other with blades like she had seen glimmers of in the movies and television. Her parents had tried to keep her away from that stuff when she was young, to protect her from violence. Little good that did. She judged it against her reality, which was battling zombies, suffering under Lysent goons, and fighting the elements outside. Maybe she was a warrior, but it was because she was a runner.

"I'm a runner. How are you feeling?"

This man was a walking corpse just yesterday. These scientists had replicated the antidote and now he was sitting with them, aware and alive. She needed to understand how he was doing as it related to how Belinda might do under the same circumstances.

"A little disconcerted," he replied, his strong face drawn into an honest worried look.

"Well, you remember the word 'disconcerted' so that's good," she replied wryly.

Audra abstained from showing her excitement, but her heart was pounding. It took all that was in her not to run out and into the corporation to demand her sister.

She almost forgot, too.

"Do you need anything?"

"I don't know. You'd think I'd be hungry, right?" he asked, confused about his body's continued contentment.

"Yes, you should eat something," chimed in Satomi. "Your body needs it whether your brain has caught up or not."

Ryder stepped out and retrieved a protein bar. She handed it to him with a grimace on her face.

"This is all we have," she said, wishing she could offer him something more special for his first meal back.

"Thank you," he said genuinely.

Audra remembered that he had not been eating the bars for years like they had. It was new to him. Hell, *eating* was new to him.

Gordon seemed to notice Ryder's hesitation, though.

"Is it bad out there?" he asked. "It was just getting started. We didn't realize what trouble we were putting ourselves into by bringing one of them in for studies. We thought we could help. I'm betting many people did the same."

Ryder and Dwyn shared how things were terrible at the start, but now everyone was rebuilding. Gordon was not surprised that the corporation was a key part in that. It made sense. They were so big before the world ended.

"So, is this outpost one of the last few to be treated?" he

asked, confused.

"No. Unfortunately, Lysent does not want to cure all the infected," said Satomi.

Gordon's face buried in on itself in confusion while Dwyn explained Lysent's role, reasoning, and the process and payment system behind waking people up.

"They've commercialized a public health crisis?"

His half-eaten protein bar hung forgotten in his hand.

"Haven't they always?" asked Ziv.

"I recognize you." Gordon blurted as if Ziv's snark had woken up that memory.

"Yes, I had just started working here. That's why we're at this lab – because I knew of its existence. I, um, survived when everything fell apart here, while we were trying to figure it all out."

"Thank you for coming back," said Gordon.

Ziv just gave a small nod, not going on about a rescue like Audra expected. While Ziv was typically a pain in the ass, maybe there was more to him than sarcasm and a keen sense of survival.

"So, if Lysent doesn't want to cure people... Why am I awake?"

"We woke you up illegally," Ryder said carefully.

They hoped Gordon would understand and appreciate. They did not know him. He might sympathize with the corporation. Gordon could need something from Lysent, like a family member, and turn them all in. He did not understand this world, but they woke him up hoping he would be a good and helpful person as they set this world on a different path.

"We stole a dose of antidote and have been working to replicate it. You were a trial subject given the replicated dose. As far as we know, you are the first unregulated awakening."

Gordon's eyebrows rose. He absentmindedly raised the protein bar to his mouth and chewed for a moment.

"Well, I always wanted to be part of a scientific breakthrough that changed how the world worked," he said, gesturing to the lab. "I never thought I'd BE the breakthrough."

Ryder and Satomi smiled. As part of the science and engineering fields, they understood. They too were excited about making scientific history. As an added bonus, their work had produced another of their kind.

"So, no one knows I'm alive?"

The entire group stole glances at each other.

"How do I know about my family? Are they alive? Where are they?"

Gordon seemed to remember his life outside the laboratory. It had taken awhile. This place must have meant a lot to him. What had become of the rest of his life?

"I have a daughter, Eliza. And, I guess, an ex-wife."

Audra weighed the pros and cons in her head. She had her biometric reader. She could sample Gordon's DNA and process it through the system. They could find out if his ex-wife or others had inquired about his status. But, a lack of inquiry could weigh heavy on someone's mind. Likewise, using her reader would tie her and this GPS location to the illegal awakening.

If Gordon wandered into a Lysent-sponsored village and asked about his family, there would be questions after so many years. Travelers were not welcome. He would be brought forth in front of a committee and questioned about his previous whereabouts. Lysent worried about others. They feared something much like themselves, large, organized, and predatory. Gordon would not be able to answer the questions satisfactorily, even with help.

"We will give Vesna, our leader, your family's names. She will get the word out, see if they are still in the area. She will help you," said Audra.

"I remember Vesna. Her husband?"

"No longer with us."

It seemed to sink in how different the world was. He did not push an urgency concerning his daughter. He had been ill for years. The world had and still did continue without him.

"Look, guys," Gordon said, looking each person in the eye before continuing. "I appreciate on a very personal level the efforts you all have taken here. I imagine this illegal process had risks, some of which you haven't even considered yet. If what you're saying about Lysent is true, and from my experiences I know it to be feasible, then I want to be an even bigger part of this. I want to help. You chose me because I looked like the scientist type, right? I am. Let me stay and let me help."

Audra was not sure if the speech was given because he felt conviction in his few hours of consciousness, or if he was playing his best card for survival. For all he knew, the world had not ended, and they were just experimenting with his body and brain. Audra felt all the suspicions she felt Gordon should have. The request was probably just his play at survival, to get on their good side - the provider of protein bars and information. Either Ziv seemed to share Audra's suspicions or he did not want another in the group. His face showed disdain. Dwyn and Satomi were not readable. Ryder seemed convinced. She grinned and nodded her head. She went to say something and Audra cut her eyes at her. Ryder changed what she was going to say.

"We will have to talk about it and decide. To be honest, we were not getting our hopes up that this trial would work. Sorry." Ryder said nervously.

She did not realize the others were not behind her.

"You'll, of course, want to get to know us before you join our group anyway," said Audra in a more diplomatic way. "We will not kick you out to the curb. Don't worry about that."

Audra tried to change the subject.

"You're probably a good fit if you know Vesna. How do you know her?"

"Her husband was a scientist here, but he went home to his family. I hoped he had made it."

This was news to Audra. Ziv wasn't their only connection to this lab. Audra recalled that Vesna had yet to visit the outpost.

"He left to care for his family. We weren't even trying to find a cure. I figured lots of facilities were working on it. We were trying to determine if the work Lysent paid us to do had played a role in the epidemic."

"What do you mean? What work were you doing here?" Satomi asked.

She glanced around at the equipment already in place and tried to imagine what could have been done.

"We had our own independent work through grants, but often we did Lysent contracts to keep the place afloat. The contracts would only be small pieces of a broader project. That way individual private labs could not figure out what the end product was."

"Standards of compartmentalization," piped in Ryder, familiar with the concept.

"We had handled RNA sequences a couple of times for Lysent. They always had viral applications, but not for any of the viruses we had. We figured out how to add a little tail of information to the RNA that was nonfunctional but served as an identification marker. It became protocol, but we didn't mention it to anyone and only used it on Lysent projects."

"Damn, you thought you'd find your work somewhere you didn't want it to be? Like… in the virus?"

Audra had never heard Satomi curse. Tagging RNA must have been an extreme measure, the procedure likely flying over Audra's head, but the implication did not. Could there be proof that Lysent caused the world's downfall?

Ziv's voice was cold.

"And that's why you brought an infected person in here and killed everyone. I told you it was a bad idea," he announced.

"Yes, we were trying to retrieve a sample of the viral infection, isolate it, and then find out if our tag was in the RNA material of the virus."

Despite the heaviness of the room, Audra hid a giggle. She remembered the words Satomi had shared with her at lunch. She joked that Ziv had not been eager to bring an infected person into the laboratory, "especially if it would be smarter and more useful than himself."

"What does it matter if it is there? Their plan succeeded," said Ziv, his snark back.

"Not everyone believes that Lysent is behind this, in fact, few believe it. They trust the corporation will get us out of this mess with rationing and governance. If we have evidence they were behind all of it, we would have a lot of leverage against them," spoke Ryder.

"Leverage to do what?" asked Satomi.

"To know and be with our loved ones. To get fair food rations and shelter. To not have the corporation hands all over everything."

"Do you guys have a cell line going?"

"No phones," said Dwyn, happy to know more than

someone in the room.

"No, no… a cell culture line we can use to isolate the virus."

Dwyn's body seemed to retreat into itself in embarrassment.

"I've been trying to immortalize a cell line," said Satomi.

Turning to Dwyn she explained, "Cells don't replicate indefinitely. But you need them to in order to do experiments like isolate a virus."

Satomi gave a sweet smile and Dwyn pulled his chest back out and nodded in understanding. Audra was not sure what to make of the interaction.

Gordon agreed to help Satomi in creating a medium to grow and isolate the virus. When they were ready, they would need a saliva sample from another infected subject.

Gordon's eyes hung heavy. He had been able to converse, maintain body posture, and be a real person, but it seemed to take a great energy expenditure. He was still recovering, no matter if he could think of and say words like 'disconcerting.' Dwyn offered to share his room as it would be comfier than the conference table that Gordon had slept on the night before in his half-zombie state.

Audra's eyes squinted a little at the offer. A surprising amount of envy and anger washed over her. She took a moment to place it. Then, she recognized Gordon's charmed life. Here, he had played around with a zombie at the start and gotten bit. Perhaps the laboratory was a gory scene, but it was a single scene he'd endured. He did not see his family get ripped apart or spend months in the woods hiding and hoping that the world would not end. He would not be unable to sleep because the office ceiling was too high. Audra fought hard and he waited in a lab.

"How are you feeling?" asked the ever medical-assessing Satomi before Gordon left the room.

"At first, I didn't know. But now I can place it. It's not pain. I've just spent the last… how many years again, did you say?… in pain. My joints and muscles - they were on fire. I felt like I was on fire," whispered Gordon.

Audra ran from the room.

Belinda could feel. And all she could feel was fire, a burning pain. Audra's mind rushed to the cabin in the woods. Belinda had had night terrors from that day on. And all of Audra now sank into the thought that Belinda was living it. She had been living it all these years.

Did Lysent know? Of course, Lysent knew! If they had awoken anyone, they knew. Lysent hid this from its people and continued to treat loved ones like currency despite their pain and suffering.

CHAPTER THIRTEEN

The group worked long hours on the three projects, isolating the virus to identify the marker, replicating the antidote, and aerosolizing it for an effective delivery system. Audra and Dwyn felt useless in most regards in the laboratory, but they supported and protected the scientists on all other fronts. They foraged for food, kept morale up, settled minor disputes (always involving Ziv), and retrieved supplies. Audra and Dwyn also took turns tagging zoms far from the laboratory, never circling it. As expected, no one had put down a deposit on a six-month rent. It didn't matter. Herders could come corral her tags for all she cared. Audra just wanted Lysent to believe this was her only choice.

More than a month passed before they sequenced the virus's genetic material, but the truth came out. Gordon's RNA marker was found in the virus's genetic material. With some paperwork and data, it was possible to show that Lysent had employed people and contracted out work to develop the virus. Breakthroughs usually led to rejoicing, but this one didn't.

For the scientists, one question remained. Why? Why would a successful company worth billions of dollars effectively destroy their customer base?

Audra would deliver their findings to Vesna. They gave her a full briefing and verbal tests afterward to make sure she knew and understood their case, front to back. Audra had learned more about RNA than she ever cared to know. She learned more about virus life cycles than she knew existed. Despite the microbiology, the premise of the proof was simple and undeniable. While the scientists wondered why, Audra wondered how. How could their group use this information for their benefit? With documents in her pack and Dwyn by her side, she ran to Vesna in hopes she would act. Was Vesna made of guts or talk?

"How did you and Vesna meet?" Audra asked Dwyn during their run.

"Vesna was my first stop when I became a tagger. She saw I was kinda lost and offered to let me stay and work for her until I was ready to set out on my own. When she saw how much I hated the system, she explained her role in the resistance network."

"Is there a leader?"

"Over Vesna? I don't think they're that organized yet, despite what Vesna would tell you. She puts on a show to protect. If we're small, we're easy to wipe out. A pervasive and large network is better. She may share this information with other towns. She may not. I hope she does."

Tears streamed down Vesna's face when she realized the gift Audra and the scientists handed to her.

"Ziv was right. Gary was right," she muttered to herself.

Gary. Gary must be her husband's name.

"Explain it again," she said to Audra.

Audra disseminated the information to Vesna in lay terms then with science to support it. She was proud of herself and her elementary school education. Sure, she might not be perfect in her explanation, but if she could understand it, others could, too.

Vesna stopped muttering to herself to give orders.

"Dwyn, you go back and help the others with the antiviral. Audra and I will take this to the corporation to get more food rations for the villagers and get the six-month hold taken off."

This is what Audra was waiting for. She could hardly believe her ears that Vesna was including the ban without her prodding.

"Why those things?" Audra dared to ask.

"It's a good starting point. We will also ask them to release the prisoners of the indentured taggers. Let the indentured decide if they want to continue their contracts. We will get concessions. In return, they can stay in charge. Then, we topple them with the antidote."

Audra's jaw dropped.

"Thank you," was all Audra could muster.

She had tried to take off with the antidote. And yet, Vesna was ignoring the betrayal and even rewarding her. But, the fire in Vesna's eyes told Audra that she had little to do with it. Vesna was after Lysent. Even she had grown impatient. She was ready to strike.

"Dwyn, please head back to the lab and help the scientists. That is the next part of the plan," requested Vesna.

Dwyn's face wrinkled. Doubt shadowed his face, but no one

sought his opinion.

"OK, but at least let me help you plan out the negotiation before I go."

* * *

Vesna threw up her hands after stumbling again through the explanation.

"School was never my strong suit. Gary was the smart one," she admitted.

They both felt it was important that Vesna present the science during the negotiation. Audra tried again to trace the connections in the material for Vesna, the same as Satomi had for her. At the end, Audra glanced to Vesna, who met her with deep set worry. Eyes that did not show concern when she sent scientists out into the wilderness or predicted that Audra would join their ranks, showed a past life of under-confidence resurfacing. Audra gave her a small squeeze around the shoulders to reassure. She set aside the paper and made her own illustrations as she talked it over once more in simpler words and fewer presumptions.

Vesna's eyes brightened up three-fourths through this new presentation and Audra could see the ideas click together in her brain. Vesna then explained it back to her, even connecting ideas mentioned in previous lectures. With a second round, she was ready to explain this to a layperson like Larange, because she herself learned it that way. It was time.

Audra wrapped a light fabric scarf around her head and face and tucked it in tight. It would not be unusual and would disguise her identity from all but the most familiar of faces. Vesna may be willing to show her hand to Lysent, but Audra was not.

Audra and Vesna walked through the plaza and up the steps to the large building. Inside Rosie sat in front as always.

"We would like an audience with Larange Greenly, please," Vesna requested.

Rosie gave a questioning look to first Vesna then Audra.

"No, that won't be possible."

"We have something of the corporation's interest. Give us the highest person you can and we will start from there," said Vesna undeterred.

"Actually," said Audra, "give us a scientist."

With some amusement, Rosie picked up the phone and pushed buttons.

"Dr. Lambert, do you have time to see a couple walk-ins?"

"Your names?" she directed toward the women.

"Ashley Williams and Veronica Peters."

Rosie recited the names through the phone, staring at Audra pointedly. Rosie had helped Audra every time she'd visited, and had seen her grow in the past 3 years like she was her own child coming back from play. She recognized her but kept her secret for now.

Rosie nodded, even though Dr. Lambert could not see, and hung up the phone.

"He will be with you shortly."

Dr. Lambert was a tall, skinny man with glasses and graying wavy hair. He smiled when he arrived at the front lobby. Without greeting, Vesna shoved the papers into his chest. His eyes squinted in confusion. He looked through the stack of papers, reading each title page and scanning its contents. After he finished his first scan, he offered nothing to Vesna or Audra.

He walked over to the front desk and spoke in hushed words to Rosie.

"It's probably a good time to tell you that this is not the only copy and we have people waiting for us," Vesna said.

She spoke disproportionately smoother and cooler than Audra's rapid heartbeat suggested.

Rosie ushered them into a conference room. Audra sat down and Vesna paced back and forth. Dr. Lambert had not followed them.

"Just sit down, V. They will make us wait uncomfortably long. You might as well settle," she said motioning to a chair next to her.

Truthfully, Vesna's pacing was making her nervous. Audra did not know how the corporation would handle this. They were probably somewhere on the other side of the door trying to figure it out as well.

Vesna agreed and just as her bottom was about to reach the chair, she jumped back up as the conference doors swung open and there stood Larange Greenly, her small petite frame dwarfed by the large entrance. It was difficult to picture her plotting the end of the world. Audra looked at her graying hair and weak frame. She could not help but wonder if they were wrong. Larange sharply turned her face and Audra saw a spark of both fire and darkness in her eyes. Her heart dropped into her stomach.

Two guards were behind Greenly, the same size and shape of the two when she'd announced the cure to the crowds. Dr. Lambert and a few others followed behind them. Audra assumed them to be officials for Greenly. Two of them were rather portly, an unusual sight considering.

Vesna did not want to give away that she jumped in fright,

so she reached over the table to shake Greenly's hand. Audra was not about to stand up and offer her hand to this evil woman. She gave a small nod, instead.

"Why are we here?" asked Greenly, her voice noncommittal, proper, and with an accent Audra couldn't place.

"These two have an interesting theory. It's a new stab of propaganda. Their theory is that the corporation started the virus. That is… what this concludes, correct?" He looked at Vesna.

"It's proof."

"And where did you get such 'proof'?" asked Greenly.

She spat the last word as if it tasted foul. Her lips cringed upward on a sour face.

"It only matters that we have it," answered Vesna weakly.

Neither Greenly nor her cohorts had sat down, as if they were uninterested in staying. They pretended they had the upper hand, even if that was not the case, and Vesna was already floundering. Vesna did not sit down either but seemed undecided about both that decision and the conversation's direction.

"We will figure out where you cobbled together this incorrect information. A nearby lab, no doubt," reported Dr. Lambert.

Audra's mind went to Dwyn and the others. If her eyes flashed fear, she reeled it back in. They needed to change the direction of this meeting now. Being the only one sitting, Audra stood up with the others.

"Look. You can do that, but it's too late. We've already got the documentation and sent it to others. You can't cover this up. Everyone will know.

"However, we are willing to work with you," Audra said.

Greenly's stance did not change. Her expression did not change. But she did not leave or open her mouth, so Audra continued.

"We think it's great you're in power. No one can do a better job. To be honest, we know the people are better off not knowing the truth about this epidemic. We just want a few changes for them."

Vesna seemed to collect herself by this point. She stood with her arms crossed, mirroring Greenly.

"We want to even out the food rations between those in the corporation and those doing meaningful jobs in the village. And everyone has a meaningful job in the village," Vesna noted.

She continued.

"We also want you to remove the six-month awakening ban and give the indentured taggers an opportunity to find different accommodations for their loved ones outside the villages. They will still owe you, but they will be able to stop the insurmountable growth of their debt.

"We think this would be best for you, too. It's better for long term stability if the worker ants are happy and busy."

"You do not want control?" she asked, her eyes shifting back and forth between the two. She even seemed to almost imperceptibly exhale.

"No, you would stay in control."

Greenly motioned with her hand and the papers were delivered upon them. She scanned through the documents, her eyebrows almost coming together, perhaps due to concentration but maybe emotion. Greenly knew something. Audra had always assumed that Greenly was an opportunistic manager of a Georgia Lysent branch, but was that all of her story? She didn't seem surprised by their accusations.

After scanning the papers, she looked up and assessed her confronters. Audra felt that same discerning gaze that had given her a reader and a contract years ago. Then, in a flash of anger, Greenly closed the distance between them. Her guards followed with a delay, taken aback.

"If I hear any rumor of *this,*" shaking the papers in their faces, "then I'll cut rations in half and shut down the awakening project altogether. You don't realize how difficult it is to keep balance in this village. You think you are suffering, but you don't know the half of it. Without my determination to do what's right to keep things going around here, we'd all be hurting. Take your stupid zombies, but you won't get rations until the debt is paid. Wake up whoever has cash. What do I care? I'm just trying to hold this HELL HOLE together."

"We appreciate your um, cooperation, considering. How do we know you will keep your word?" Vesna asked.

"I will make an announcement now," said Greenly.

She turned to her assistants and barked, "Gather the people."

"No gratefulness to the leaders..." she muttered as she spun on her heel to leave.

* * *

"I am pleased to announce that due to some great successes in farming, we are able to increase the food rations. This will mean less scavenging and trading. With this added abundance, I have rethought the six-month re-awakening ban. We will go back to a case-by-case basis. I realized what a strain it was for everyone, especially the taggers who do such good work for us.

"Whoever stole the antidotes," she looked at Audra and Vesna, "shouldn't ruin it for everyone."

Another official, one of the portly women who accompanied

Greenly during negotiation, took over the speech as Greenly walked away from the large noises of the crowd. She explained that taggers could come in the next week to fill out paperwork to pull out their person if they no longer wanted Lysent to render care.

"We want no one to feel stuck."

Audra smirked at the statement. That was exactly what the indentured tagging program was. The woman made clear that money would be owed with interest compounding, but they would not use humans as collateral, only giving the option of care. Other fees would apply. After out-processing, they would be available at the end of the week.

Audra waited a few days before arriving with her paperwork. She presented it to Rosie with a big smile on her face. Rosie gave a timid smile back. Audra hadn't shown Rosie any appreciation for not revealing her identity, even if it ended up not mattering. She softened her smile and mouthed, "thank you." Rosie nodded and accepted her paperwork. It landed in a large pile on her desk. Audra knew better than to argue. Rosie wouldn't mess up something so important.

Audra refrained from asking how many applications had been dropped off. She knew several taggers who were on the verge of giving up and some who had, leaving the township system entirely. Audra knew she would owe near a million credits, but she would have her sister. She would wake her up with a replicated antidote. And if they could incite Lysent's fall, this system of debt and her debt would be no more. Audra knew a lot had to go right, but it was the same as signing on as a tagger had been. For that, nothing had gone right. At least this time, she had more control.

Audra stepped outside to renewed protests. No longer on a

six-month break, it seemed they were just as upset over removing the infected from the village as they were with waking them up. Releasing zombies near the towns, allowing people to keep them in their homes? They didn't care that the announcement stated that the infected could not stay in the township. Too many dead, unsafe and worthless, they argued, ignoring that others saw them as loved, curable, and important.

The infected were people. They deserved a chance, no matter how hard the community struggled. Or in Audra's case, how much she personally struggled. She couldn't imagine the possibility of her sister awake and talking by this time next week. Audra disappeared more than a few times. The moonshiners' spots were calling her name. She shook and paced in front, but she needed to stay upright to take care of her sister. Instead, she marched out of the town and went for runs, down easy roads, up harsh terrain, and coasted on rolling hills.

The next week, Audra arrived in the crowd, unsure if she was supposed to receive her sister at a specific location. Perhaps the infected would be escorted out of the town. Vesna was invited to stand with Greenly on stage as an act of good faith and collaboration. Vesna stood somber, realizing this was a business transaction, not a victory. Guards herded ten infected out into the plaza with linen sacks over their heads, all loosely bound together by their upper and lower extremities so they could walk on their own.

Audra heard the protesters gasp and squeal.

"What if they get out of control?" they whispered.

Even with Belinda in the mix, Audra let out a giggle at the thought of a mass of tangled zombies wreaking havoc on this stupid little town and its stupid little protesters. Audra tried to figure out which one was Belinda. There were a few the correct height and skin tone, but the formless white uniforms and linen sacks covering face and hair revealed little else.

Looking through the crowd, Audra spotted a few taggers here to receive or possibly just observe. No one tried to approach the chained. Taggers were a cautious bunch, and it wasn't zombies they feared. Greenly stepped up to the podium with Vesna on her left side, and even the protesters observed their place in society by falling silent for their leader.

"Welcome. You all have been doing a wonderful job building our community and making sure there is food for all. Your successes have brought us increased rations. You did that. Now we can all be that much more productive.

"There is one of our own. Perhaps you know her. This is Vesna. Vesna runs a little shop for the corporation. You have probably bought from her before. Vesna approached me and requested that I end the six-month waiting period and release any zombies whose loved ones did not wish to be part of the program anymore. And just last week I did that."

Greenly and Vesna looked a lot alike, petite women with graying hair. Both seemed weathered from the infection that swept the nation, but one of them was responsible for it.

"But, the six-month waiting period was imposed because an individual stole from us. One person hurt many because he or she demanded something for themselves. And the indentured tagging program exists because you must help others before you can help yourself - whether that is by giving money to further our lives here or by helping to wake up others. You cannot demand for just yourself anymore."

Audra's eyes widened and she hoped to make eye contact with Vesna. Vesna shifted on her feet and looked to the side of the stage. Doubt and panic filled both of their bodies. Vesna made a footstep to stage left, but two guards stepped forward and sandwiched her. Something was wrong. Audra worked her way around the crowd and to the stage.

"This woman is demanding for herself. She is not trying to help us. She is trying to hurt us."

Greenly gave a small nod and one of the large arms of a guard grabbed Vesna. Her arms were pinched to her sides, but she struggled all the same. He pulled out his gun and with a quick move to the temple, he executed Vesna. Vesna slumped to the ground in the midst of gasps and cries. This was unlike anything Lysent had ever done in public view. What positive public opinion her speech had garnered was lost in the display of violence. With no thoughts clearing her mind, Audra doubled over in shock and a measure of less oxygen.

Then, another smatter of noise. This time, multiple weapons.

Audra looked up to all ten in linen collapsing to the ground.

"We will no longer bow to the individual!" Greenly shouted.

And with that, the crowd was on her side once again. Cheers erupted.

Audra did not hear them as she too fell to the ground. Her ears rang with death. She screamed out with no release. Soon, she was forced to suck in, but she received only dust into her lungs. She rubbed her face on the ground as she attempted another yell out. What had she done?

Audra felt a warm hand grab her shoulder. She turned to push away the intruder but saw a familiar face she could not place. The soft face came down to her and her lips brushed her hair and ear as she whispered.

"I didn't put in your paperwork. Your sister is safe inside."

It was Rosie.

Audra froze on the ground, eyes wide, trying to process the

information.

"Get up," Rosie ordered with a hoarse whisper. "Your laboratory is in danger. She knows where it is. They're going to destroy all evidence of whatever it is you brought, of you, of anyone who knows."

"How?" she choked.

"They're sending a herd."

Her sister was OK. She was not here in the mass of white and red? But Dwyn and the others? Vesna. Vesna gone. Her mind refused to wrap around to connect all the thoughts, but she reached a conclusion all the same. She pulled herself off the ground and without a word, a look back, or a brushing off of the smeared agony on her body, she ran.

CHAPTER FOURTEEN

The paths were empty. Everyone was still gathered in Lysent's plaza, not yet dismissed. Audra raced to their small outpost in this town. There, Audra and Vesna had packed bags in case something went wrong. And something had.

Audra would not be able to tote both bags. She opened Vesna's, retrieving a few things. As she did, a shadow came into the room. Someone was here. She whipped out her knife. Only Vesna knew this spot. And Vesna… she was gone. She rushed the shadow's origin.

"No no no, it's me," came Dwyn's voice.

She slacked her knife arm and fell into him. Her emotions smashed into his. He knew. He had just arrived, but he had seen. Then, he had chased her here. She buried herself in him and spoke into his chest.

"She, she, my sister... She wasn't in the group," she breathed. Was that true? Dwyn wasn't sure. Maybe that was just shock or denial. It didn't matter in this moment. He needed to get Audra out of here. If Lysent identified her, she'd be dead.

"And, Rosie. An attack, an attack on the lab. A herd."

That. That made perfect sense to Dwyn.

"OK, we need weapons then."

Now they could bring both bags. Audra moved to reveal their contents - traps, knives, flares, noisemakers, all manners of self-defense. With emotions still churning, they took off with their loot while the rest of the town still reeled in the square.

"The laboratory is this way," Dwyn said, attempting to guide Audra.

"We're not going there yet."

"What do you mean?" he asked but followed her all the same. Her head seemed to clear now that she was in the forest and on her feet.

"We're going to the corral."

Dwyn had never seen one. Even with his extra gear, he picked up his pace in anticipation even with his extra gear.

Vesna's goal had been to wake up the surrounding corrals. Lysent's goal was now to weaponize them by releasing them to kill people. Why not? Lysent controlled food, construction, and now were making public displays of murder. The villagers didn't care as long as it was in the name of safety and security. Vesna had seen how urgently Lysent needed to be stopped. She had prioritized accountability, which made even more special, her forgiveness of Audra's detour.

Audra's heart ached with the memory.

Dwyn interrupted her thoughts with something that had been weighing on his mind.

"Your sister? You think she is still alive?"

His timidity in speech gave away that he still didn't believe.

"That's what Rosie said," she replied with a harshness that ended the conversation.

Audra wasn't sure she believed it either, but she couldn't let go of the prospect. She had to hold onto Rosie's words. If they weren't true, Audra would fall apart and more people would die. And she couldn't let that happen. Her family was more than just Belinda now. It was the entire group. She wasn't going to lose anyone else.

But the guilt of Vesna's death covered, like paint, every thought she had. Every possible blame and future scenario flooded Audra's head as she stomped through the brush.

She distracted herself with endless pace calculations. The corral was ten miles east. The shepherds on horses would arrive in the morning to release and direct the zoms. They would move more slowly than Audra and Dwyn, but would not rest at night. Still, it would take two full days at least. They would possibly arrive in time for a nightfall attack.

Audra picked up the pace to give everyone more time to prepare.

The soft intermittent sirens told Audra they were close, and they slowed to a walk. It was not a good idea to rile up a herd. As they crested the hill, they caught sight of the corral, an expansive pen with close to five hundred zoms. Even from this distance, Audra's trained tagging eye could assess their condition. Exposed to weather and to each other, their skin sagged, muscles shredded, and bones stuck this way and that. They had torn and gnawed on each other. Flaps of skin and tufts of hair clung to the chain-link fences, pulled from their hosts.

Audra knew Belinda did not have the accommodations Lysent boasted, but at least she hadn't been left to this.

Dwyn let out a low whistle and then a curse.

"They're all coming to us?" asked Dwyn.

Audra looked at the five hundred as a mass. She imagined them destroying the forest as they came like an unstoppable ocean wave.

"No, no, not for our little place. They wouldn't. It would be unsafe to have all these zoms running around after they plowed through our laboratory," scrambled Audra, half convincing herself.

The scientists would be frightened beyond belief. Dwyn looked scared, too.

"Why do they look like that?"

"Lysent packed them all in together and left them."

"These are just chain-link fences. How have they not…I don't know… stampeded out?"

"Listen. Hear that siren? In a few minutes, it'll stop and another one will replace it coming from a different direction. They keep them going in circles, so they don't weigh on the fence."

"So, they direct them?"

"Sorta."

"And now they're going to direct them right into our lab?"

"Not all of them. Maybe fifty. A hundred?" Audra tried to estimate.

"I think we can handle fifty. Much more and we'd get overrun."

"That's why we're here."

"We set them loose?"

"Yes."

Releasing the corral prematurely might call off the attack. All hands would be needed to round up the zombies. Or, maybe not. Maybe hundreds more would be directed toward them, simply because they were available.

Despite her affirmation, neither made a move toward the corral. By ripping open select fences, they could split the herd and choose their general trajectories. It mitigated the risk to others but promised nothing. Zombies would stumble into the townships, onto people's paths, and increase the ill favor that the infected garnered.

They sat waiting for an answer to manifest. The bodies were walking corpses. Only the virus's grip on their metabolisms kept them alive. Without it, they would pass from their injuries. Death would be more merciful, but they did not have time. There were hundreds and Lysent was purposely keeping them alive.

"Vesna would release them," Dwyn concluded.

She would. Given her way, she would have brought them to Lysent's fences and she would have mass-cured them. She would let them all writhe and die in front of those who swore to protect and care.

"We're not Vesna."

Audra pulled away from their hiding place and headed toward the lab, corral untouched. They did not bother to cover their tracks. A giant herd would be on the way soon.

Audra pulled more food from her pack and encouraged Dwyn to do the same. It was crucial to stay ahead of the energy expenditure. Accessible food energy allowed you to run. Without it, your body had to convert fat stores. In twenty miles, you'd be forced to walk. Their pace might still be unsustainable. She hoped that adrenaline and salty snacks would see them through.

Her legs felt like concrete and she felt a snapping pain on her hip with each step. She reminded herself that the sooner she reached the laboratory, the longer she would have to rest. And even if she arrived useless and spent, the scientists would have warning. For now, they had no idea.

Dwyn and Audra ran by moonlight to reach the gate of the facility. After fifty miles, Audra's priority was still telling the others about the impending attack, but a disproportionate second priority was raiding their food supply. With just fifty yards left, their bodies demanded they walk.

The scientists jumped at the sight of their runners. Dwyn had left them just last night to support Audra and Vesna.

Good news never traveled this fast.

"What happened?"

Audra opened her mouth to speak, but no words came out. In the day of running, she had not considered how she would share the news, that she had been wrong, that Vesna had been wrong, that Vesna was dead. Soon, she found words, but they were not graceful or soothing. Confusion and sadness mingled in their wake.

What would they do without their leader? Leave? Surrender?

And they had lost a friend.

"I told you they would figure it out," came Ziv's smug brag.

Despite her complete bodily exhaustion, Audra still had to hold herself back from socking him in the jaw. Audra contented herself knowing that he was in the same path of harm despite his condescending mouth.

"What do we do?" asked Ryder.

Ryder, the one full of answers and ideas, had been confronted with a problem that overwhelmed her. She looked panicked. They all looked panicked.

"I know this attack is scary, but we have notice and time to figure something out. You guys need to finish any time-sensitive stuff. Then we'll buckle down and get ready for a siege, of sorts."

"About that 'time-sensitive stuff'…" said Satomi.

She motioned to the conference room window to reveal an infected man circling the table.

"Subject Four is our first aerosolized delivery," Gordon reported.

"Gordon and Ziv are working on that. Satomi and I are systematizing antiviral production," explained Ryder.

Audra had only thought of the human occupants of the laboratory when she rushed over, but now she realized all of their work was in jeopardy, too. Without the lab, Belinda would remain where she was, how she was. Lysent was sending a herd to destroy old evidence and any chance for her sister. With the fog of the corporation's promises lifted, Audra knew she would never get her sister through tagging.

The crew had stopped talking. Audra looked up and realized they were waiting for her approval.

"That's great," muttered Audra.

"How did you get him in there?" Dwyn asked, pointing to Subject Four.

"It was Gordon," said Satomi.

She gave Gordon a sweet smile, and he blushed in return.

The zombie was clad in a jumpsuit, perhaps a member of the maintenance crew. Audra wondered if he would wake in time to help them in the attack, but she did not voice the hope.

"Not much you can do about him. Let's first put away

anything sensitive or fragile," suggested Audra.

She looked around at the various glassware and equipment strewn about the laboratory. Perhaps there was a method to their madness, but it looked like a herd had already passed through. Ziv wandered away, muttering about having to stop his experiment. Something about incubation time and additional variables. Audra looked over to Ryder to see how serious this was. Ryder just shook her head. Ziv was just creating drama, unaware of the drama unfolding around him.

Audra's body needed rest, but she did not want to abandon the scientists. She settled for water, food, and stretching out on the tile floor. The scientists were full of questions as they worked to clean up the lab. How far was the herd? How fast did a herd move? How many shepherds? Audra offered answers as she could and speculated on the rest.

Damn her calves were tight.

She tried to get everyone to bed early. The herd would be another two days, but sleep deprivation would hurt them sooner.

In the morning, Audra tested her body. Her legs felt shredded and her step tendered by blisters, but there was no joint pain, no dehydration headache. She counted her current recovery path as successful and grabbed a protein bar to repair her muscles.

She glanced in on Subject Four. Unlike Gordon who had paced, he stood motionless. The badge on his jumper had been torn and neither Ziv nor Gordon could recall a name. Audra asked if the process would be slower, given the delivery method. They all shrugged their shoulders. Doubt shadowed Ryder's face. Gordon joked that he himself was exceptional, but everyone agreed it was possible that Subject Four had not gotten an effective dose.

Audra was shocked to find the sun was two hours old. Daylight was lost by sleeping indoors, but the sleep had done her good. Without her, the scientists had eaten breakfast and finished storing away crucial supplies for their experiments. Audra hoped the zombies would not breach this room at all, but the precautions were necessary. Their work needed to be kept safe.

Audra set up some desks as fortification inside the laboratory. If zombies or people came in, they would have a choke point and fortifications to defend their space.

"I understand keeping the equipment safe, but shouldn't we clear out of here before they come?" asked Dwyn.

Audra shook her head.

"A few tents will not protect us from a passing herd. We need to protect our home and the research. We can't find a new lab or steal more antidote. That won't work again," said Audra.

They were safer inside, even if that was where their enemies wanted them to be. Audra sent the scientists to gather what they wanted from their sleeping quarters. They would stay and protect the lab only. It could be a week or more after the initial attack before they could move freely. Gordon took inventory and stockpiled food in the cabinet. Ziv was tasked with gathering as much water as possible. He stopped up the defunct sinks and filled them with water for drinking. Any clean container was filled.

Audra and Dwyn found two cars and positioned them on either side of the gate to block it when ready. Audra wished they had lined up vehicles along the facility's perimeter as soon as they had moved in, but it would have given away their presence.

Now that they were found, they didn't have time. Dwyn cut the barbed wire off the top of the back fence and laid it in front of the gate as the others created more snares. Audra and Satomi cut down small saplings with hatchets and sharpened each end, one to bury into the ground and the other to stick out and skewer the zombies. If they could snare a good portion, Dwyn and Audra could kill the rest. Ziv placed the sapling spears into the ground. He complained that they were not using his brain to its full potential, and instead were having him do hard labor. Audra asked him to think of other fortifications they could build with their limited time and resources as he worked. He seemed content with that responsibility, and came up with approximately zero ideas as he dug.

Satomi had a unique job. After the attack, the shepherds would come on their horses and assess the damage. Audra wanted the place to appear destroyed, defeated, and overrun. Satomi opened the windows of all the other buildings, marking the exterior walls near the door frames and windows with ash to resemble burned-out buildings. She scattered debris from the buildings into the yard to distract the assessors. Satomi pulled even more sick ones from storage to plant around the plaza. Their movement might rile the herd but would discourage the riders from coming too near.

Ryder was given most of the noisemakers Dwyn and Audra had brought. She strung them together electronically and set them to a radio frequency to remotely control them. Dwyn and Ryder ran a mile west to set them up. Gordon gave great praise of Ryder's engineering, praise which she did not notice.

Two days of work and this evening's dinner didn't fill the time left to wait for the mass of deteriorating people. Nightfall might bring their arrival, but Audra imagined it would be closer to dawn before they caught sight of their attackers. Audra attempted to prepare the scientists for what they were about to face. These infected were real people but largely destroyed. Even if they had antidotes to give, the zoms would wake up in tremendous amounts of pain. They had lost skin, faces, and limbs. They would not survive as humans again. Their lives as scientists were more important. They said they understood and Audra hoped when the time came they would depersonalize the sick, and not get swept up by the horror they faced. Nervous composure filled the lab. Gordon offered to take first watch.

It was well past midnight when Satomi pushed on Audra's shoulder. Audra's eyes popped open, but Satomi was already heading to her bed. Her lack of a report said everything. Audra removed herself from all but one blanket. She pulled it along with her, also grabbing her jacket. Once she had navigated around the sleepers, she stretched from head-to-toe before slipping on her jacket and draping the blanket over her shoulders. In the front office, she settled into the chair pushed close to the window, which had been boarded up except for a small slit. She looked into the courtyard. Their tethered zombies rocked, but otherwise remained motionless, a sort of zombie sleep. The darkness and lack of visual stimuli allowed rest for them. Past them, the moonlight bounced off the chain-link fence. Audra cracked the front door open and was met with the sound of frogs and the breeze through the trees. The cicadas had quieted since the weather had cooled. The draft hit the back of her neck and Audra retreated further into the blanket. Nothing moved past the fences. Audra waited as part of the night.

An hour and a little more passed with nothing to be seen. Audra walked back into the laboratory and woke Ziv. He only had 45 minutes left in his shift. He could pay it forward or wake up the next person if he was tired.

"Thank you" came the whisper, surprising Audra.

Ziv had slept in his jacket, so it was already warm. He, too, dragged a blanket behind him. Audra returned to her confined space, sandwiched between a counter and Dwyn. She pulled blankets over her head to create a tent. She may have drifted off, but she was undecided on that point when Ziv came in with rushed whispers. He could see things moving out there.

Ryder threw off her blankets and jumped up. The others were fast behind her. Audra moved deliberately slowly and encouraged everyone to do the same. Rushing around would not help anything. They did not want to draw attention to their building or swell into a panic inside. She directed Satomi to roll up the bedding and place it in the corner. No one would sleep now, even if it was a false alarm. She asked Ryder to check that everyone had two knives, one to use and one to lose. With her requests in place, she followed Ziv to confirm his sighting.

The front room was dark except for the moonlight through the boards. Audra looked past the fence. Yes, there was movement. Ziv was correct. Someone, a lot of someones, moved through the forest toward them. Audra wished it was not so dark. She could not count how many bodies were heading their way, just that they were coming.

She called for Dwyn and Ryder to judge their location relative to the noisemakers. Sounding off the noisemakers at the optimal time would distract a good number of them away from the facility. Soon they were all in the front room, waiting. Once Ryder determined it was time, Dwyn sent the radio signal.

A tornado siren blared in the west accompanied by three successive flares into the sky. Ryder did a few silent fist pumps as the noise pierced the night. It was impossible to tell how many were leaving and how many were still heading for them. The motion of the trees highlighted by the moon was their only reference, but there was no way all the zoms were still heading their way with the lure in place. Everyone gave Ryder a pat on the back. With the siren blaring a mile away and the anticipation of the zoms hitting the first snares of barbed wire and tin cans, Audra knew requesting that the others sleep was a futile effort. They sat and rested, but no one dozed.

CHAPTER FIFTEEN

In lieu of sleep, Audra ordered everyone to eat at sunrise. When the sirens stopped during breakfast, Ryder could not confirm if they had run their course or if someone had shut them off. The new quiet soon gave way as the first zombies tripped over the knee-high tin can and barbed wire contraption in front of the plaza. It would stop the ones on the front line, but not the rest. A large herd would fill up the barbed wire with bodies and others would climb over.

As the sun rose and more arrived, it became clear the herd was massive. Near a hundred zoms approached, crawling over those caught. Some tangled in the wire did not stay, leaving clothes and skin behind. They hit the stakes next, of which there were not enough. Audra watched as a burly zom levered the spear that bored into him. He now approached with a skewer lodged in his chest. Some worked as planned, the stick going straight through their chest cavity and out the other side. Struggling just pushed them farther onto the skewer, leaving room on the other side for another.

The mass of dead kept coming, past the spikes, up against the cars and fence. The crew watched the drove of torn bodies, jagged limbs, and hanging gray flesh. Their laboratory zoms pulled at their tethers toward the visitors, making wide arm motions. Visitors, two layers deep, leaned on the fences. The chain-links bent and bowed.

"Should we go protect the fence?" asked Gordon.

"I think we should leave," muttered Ziv.

Ziv pointed to pockets of denser numbers creating weak points in the fence. The gate was pulling open from the pressure on either side. No one had managed through, but it was only a matter of time. The fence would fall. The gate would tear open.

Audra looked but feared more intelligent enemies, who might use the zoms as a distraction for a bigger plan. Would they have firearms or explosives? Audra imagined a grenade attack would make short work of the laboratory. Although there were so many infected and riled, it did not matter. No ammunition needed. This place would be torn down.

"If we leave, we'll lose the antidotes," explained Satomi for the third time.

Audra broke the news.

"We can't go out and kill them. The fence will come down before we get them all."

"What do we do?" asked Ryder.

Audra wasn't sure. She examined the situation. Lysent had gathered a sick population and left them in the elements to rot. Then, instead of killing them, they used them to kill others. Their consideration for humanity was vitriolic. Maybe Belinda was right about this new world. Audra shook the thought from her head. Looking past the philosophy, their group could also use the zombies to intimidate and destroy. They just needed to redirect them.

"We will move them."

Dwyn looked at her to assess her seriousness.

"We send them to the township," she said.

"Audra…" Dwyn hesitated.

"We've caught a good many. Lysent will handle them well before they wreak havoc on the town's walls. If not, maybe people will wake up to what is happening."

"It's a good idea in theory, but how are we," he motioned to the group who already looked scared at the prospect of doing anything more than killing a handful through the fence, "how are we going to move them? And possibly under the nose of herders?"

"We jump over the back fence. We get behind the zoms, start up some noisemakers, and run toward the township."

"I could run awhile," said Satomi timidly. "I ran track in high school. I could get a mile."

Gordon nodded, signaling he would help.

"I'm not leaving here. That is truly a stupid idea," said Ziv.

He crossed his arms, not averting his eyes from the horror that Audra was asking him to engage.

Ryder looked at the others, trying to decide.

"Do we need all of us to do the run? Could we do it if Ziv refused to go?" she asked.

Ziv looked offended that they would continue without him. He meant to squash the whole plan, not be the only one in the safety of the lab.

"Sure. Dwyn and I would run the inside lanes. Gordon will be just out from us. You and Satomi would be the perimeter runners," she replied, and knowing Ziv's approval would sway the others, she added, "Ziv, you could deal with any zombies that clung to the fence after."

Ziv seemed to like that idea and did not press his first opinion.

"I think Vesna would agree to this plan," shared Dwyn.

Audra wasn't sure if that was an encouragement or a deterrent. Ryder watched the fence sway, her mind doing engineering calculations.

"Well, let's get to it then," she confirmed.

They would be within chain-shouting distance of one another, but still, Audra hastily equipped everyone with a flare and a small pack along with their noisemakers. The pack would not hinder their running but would give them enough supplies to last a couple of days if they got separated.

"Only use the flare tomorrow morning if you get lost. Then head east where the sun rose. The flare will attract the zoms," she warned.

"I might not be able to take care of all the infected on the fence. There will be plenty not drawn away," discussed Ziv, not even giving others time to ask questions about their riskier roles.

Audra and Dwyn climbed over the empty back fence where Dwyn had removed the barbed wire. They helped the other three down.

"Good luck," called Ziv on the other side.

He seemed scared on all fronts - too scared to go with them and too scared to be alone. Ryder gave one last look to Satomi, blinking but trying to stay focused before Audra escorted Satomi and Gordon around one side of the plaza and Ryder went with Dwyn to the other.

Audra led her two a good deal away from the compound.

They would need to get around the crowd without being seen prematurely. Audra continued to listen for sounds of herders, and watched for signs of their presence. She saw none and hoped that Dwyn found the same lack of signs. Perhaps the herders had gone home to rest their horses and themselves before coming back to assess the damage. Everyone who worked under the corporation desired shelter and safety. Audra never saw a corporation worker out in the field for long unless they were indentured. The group could use their dependency on comfort to their advantage.

Near a thousand meters away from the laboratory, Audra saw Dwyn and Ryder again. She had left Satomi at a similar distance on the edge and Gordon between them. Satomi and Gordon would both be in the rough brush but would have less distance to sweep when it came time to break away. Audra could see that Dwyn had pulled out his noisemaker. It was time. The others would know soon enough. On the noisemakers went.

The sound emitted from Audra's device settled on a pitch between a tornado siren and a rescue whistle, but screeched like an alarm clock. In between the pauses, she heard Dwyn's more soothing chop-chop helicopter noise. The others joined in, but fainter. They were already running. Audra and Dwyn waved the devices over their heads, the sound swinging from ear to ear. They jumped up and down. More than just a novel noise, they wanted to be bait. The zoms turned from the fence and toward the runners. Audra and Dwyn smiled at each other and pulled away. The noisemakers had enough battery power for about half an hour. When the last one turned off, they would know to run to their respective sides and out of sight.

Audra's turned off shortly after Dwyn's. She set it down and then returned to it, second guessing for the ringing in her ears.

Eventually, all the noise was just a faint echo in her head. Audra looked back to the zoms careening toward her. The long run to the lab was two days ago and though she could still feel it in her quads, she was ready to run again. Quick stepping around roots gave her a rhythm that nothing else did. She ran farther and faster until she was out of sight. She then veered east to get around them. She caught up with Gordon. Despite his previous zombie state, he had an innate strength he had shown several times already. This run was no exception, although his recovery would be slow. Together, they found Satomi and ran back, having escaped the herd. Satomi was both pleased with her running performance and her sense of direction. Audra shared that she would make a good tagger with conditioning. Satomi smiled under her bangs and they walked and ran in intervals back to the facility. They hoped Dwyn and Ryder were doing the same on the other side.

Audra was pleased to see that the place was still standing. There was activity, but just of the sick on spikes, on the ground, trying to gain footing once more. The sick wandered this way and that, their attention being drawn in too many directions. Their clothing and skin hung in equal proportions off the bone. While it was chaos, it was slow chaos and easy to see that there were no shiny new corpses amongst the army.

She smiled when she saw the front gate was still crowded. They would find Ziv inside and comfortable with some excuse. They got to the back fence and threw their packs over. It looked like they had beaten Ryder and Dwyn.

Satomi was already talking about how hungry she was. Running had that effect on people. Audra smiled. They would go eat with Ziv and talk strategy on how to clear the fence. She also wanted to suggest a move. Lysent might continue to monitor this location. It was best to take their equipment and settle elsewhere. Her sister was another subject to discuss. Surely the scientists would understand the danger she was in now that they had experienced it for themselves.

From the front lobby, Satomi and Gordon entered the lab ahead of Audra. As they crossed the threshold, a flash of color filled up the doorway and pushed the two out of sight. Someone had blindsided them both. Audra sidestepped and braced herself against the wall. Her knife found her hand.

Why the hell was she so stupid? There was a reason Ziv was nowhere to be found, not just because he was lazy.

"Come on in here. We have your friends now. Nothing you can do but get one of them killed if you don't show your face," said an unknown voice from within the lab.

"What do you want?" she asked buying time.

"We're just going to take you to headquarters. We have a nicer lab, less zombies."

The voice moved something inside Audra, but she did not know what. Did she know him?

"Are the three of you all right in there?" Audra asked, seeking more information.

"The three of us are fine. These two haven't hurt us yet."

So, there were just two in there. Audra scraped the number "2" into the wood panel as quietly as possible. She pushed her knife in between the panels to punctuate it, hoping Dwyn would see it in time. She then raised her arms above her head and pivoted around so she was in front of the lab entrance.

"OK, I'm coming in."

"Good job, now sit down there and keep your arms up."

The spindly cowboy held Gordon with one arm, the other hand wielding a switchblade. He motioned to a chair for Audra before tying Gordon up and leaving him seated on the floor, several feet away from the whimpering, half-leaning Ziv. The man sauntered up to Audra. He looked at her face and his expression changed. Audra did not recognize him, but he appeared to recognize her. His grin got wide and his eyes sparkled.

"Shit, Lars. We've met this one before."

He grabbed her outstretched wrists and zip-tied them together behind her chair. He pivoted the chair on its back legs, presenting Audra. Audra imagined that if they still had football teams, Lars would be on one. He was wide, strong, and without a neck. He was an overwhelming presence in the room.

"Geez, we have!" he said.

Hearing their voices together reignited Audra's memories, too. These were the voices she heard after she'd been knocked out by the car door on I-16.

"Is this level 2 now?" asked the large guy anxiously. He hugged Satomi with one large arm over her arms and breasts and the other around her waist, but he looked at Audra greedily.

Gordon jumped up and charged into the man that had secured Audra. They both ended up on the floor in the struggle, but Gordon was at a disadvantage. A few hard punches into the side of his jaw left him slack.

"Thanks for the help, Lars," the man snarled.

He pulled himself off the floor, favoring his left knee.

"Aw, you had it, Lindon," Lars said with his arms still around Satomi.

Lindon tied Gordon's feet and dragged the unconscious body into the closet.

They returned to their conversation.

"Well, I guess since this is our second meeting, by default, it IS level 2, Lars."

He tied each of Audra's ankles to one of the chair legs. Out of desperation, Audra considered biting the top of his head but did not think that would help. The two looked strong, and Satomi was the only one not tied up. They would have to buy time until Dwyn and Ryder arrived to change their odds.

Large motion caught her eye. She looked over at the conference room. Subject Four was writhing in front of the window, foaming at the mouth. The duo looked to see what Audra was watching.

"Why you got this one?" asked Lars.

He looked around the room for a volunteer, but no one offered an answer. Had he been told why he was sent here? The terms they used like 'Level 1 and 2 encounters' led Audra to believe they were privy to nothing. Lars squinted his eyes as he came to his own conclusion.

"Well, you're scientists. *That* looks like an experiment," he said.

He tapped on the window. Subject Four did not respond, yet he seemed overstimulated, perhaps even having a seizure. His eyes closed, and he slid down to the floor.

"Wow, you guys are sick."

He walked away from the window and turned his attention to Ziv, who had found his rear and was sitting up against the wall.

"Do you want to watch?" he asked Ziv.

"Psh, we should make him join in. I bet he'd be enthusiastic after a while," said Lindon.

Ziv stared down into his lap, afraid to ask what he would be watching. Nobody said anything. Satomi now lay hogtied on her side on the floor. Audra shot glares at the closet door that hid Gordon. He had disadvantaged himself so much. He made no noise in the closet. He was either still knocked out or he had realized his mistake.

Despite the discussion, it seemed to be just idle talk for now. Audra was not sure why the men waited. Were they waiting for Dwyn and Ryder or more from their own team? The two men perched themselves on the laboratory counters. Lindon kept alert, hands on each side of his hips ready to spring up into action. His dark eyes read the room, and he swung his greasy hair out of his face. Lars pulled his legs up onto the counter and jammed himself into a corner. He barely kept his eyes off Audra, who sat spread on the chair.

Dwyn and Ryder would arrive soon. Would they heed the warning signs? Audra tried to glance nonchalantly out the window looking for any hint that the duo was out there and making a plan.

"Looking for your friends?"

Audra's eyes shot to the speaker too quickly.

"That chick and your boy? Must have found something fun to do in the woods…" he trailed off as he made a crude gesture.

He must have watched them jump the fence and let them move the zombies. Why? And were they being taken to Lysent or were they going to be executed here? Audra imagined that even if a trip to Lysent was on the horizon, a trial and execution would also be.

Shouting came from outside and disturbed the pair on the counters. Lindon and Lars jumped down. Lindon walked to the front room to investigate. Lars remained behind to watch the prisoners. He pulled out his knife and traced it high along

Satomi's thigh. Satomi whimpered and pulled away, her face hidden by the fall of her black hair. Audra listened hard to the noises outside.

It was Dwyn.

"Audra! Audra! It's Ryder! Oh god, we got overrun! She's gone! My leg… I think it's broken."

"So you're the only one left. Come inside before I kill the others."

"Argh, we've got a runner," Lindon yelled into the lab. "Come help, Lars! I ain't running after him myself."

Lars cursed under his breath.

"Did you threaten to kill his loved ones?"

"Guess he don't love them much," called out Lindon.

Lars chuckled at the crew and headed out the door. It was the first time they were left by themselves, but it wouldn't do much good. Audra pulled on her bindings, but they only pinched tight on her skin. Was Dwyn providing a distraction or had something horrible really happened to Ryder? Satomi was crying.

A head peeked from the doorway - Ryder.

"Me first!" cried Audra, her tone somewhere in the broad spectrum of a fierce command and a pathetic cry. Ryder obeyed and snipped the hard plastic zip ties that constrained Audra before rushing to Satomi and holding her. Audra jumped up as soon as she felt the freedom gather around her wrists and ankles. Without a word to the others, she made a direct line to the door to chase the men chasing Dwyn. Dwyn's actions had freed her, but she would not let him fight them alone. She crashed through the front lobby, turning to jerk her knife from the wall. She had enough. She didn't want to know what a level 3 encounter was, but she did want them to regret pushing that door into her months ago. She launched through the front door, readying her sprint to Dwyn.

BAM!

Audra hit something hard. A human arm was braced in front of the door in anticipation for someone Audra's size to come barreling through. Audra felt the back of her head smack the floor and stars floated through her vision. The owner of the clothesline maneuver, Lars, filled up the doorway, solid and angry. He must have assumed subterfuge and had doubled back. Despite the fog in her brain, she did not lose her determination to leave. She rolled away and pulled herself up. She thought for a moment about attacking Lars, but she remembered that was ill-advised. He was at least twice Audra's size. Audra was no match, no matter her enthusiasm. He was an employed goon, paid to be a fighter. Audra was paid to run.

Lars took his time entering the lobby, pleased with his power and in no hurry to run after Dwyn.

"You think I'm that dumb? I'm taking you all back for my payday."

"I get that, but didn't you ever stop to think about *why* Lysent wants us? We're trying to create antivirals here, but Lysent wants to keep control."

She backed up into the laboratory.

"Let them have control. I like it here."

Audra looked around. The second door had been barred shut, a poor decision on their part. The only other escape routes were the windows. Audra grabbed the centrifuge, much to Satomi's disagreement, and threw it through the window and followed it, cutting her arms and legs in the process.

It was not until she was a hundred yards away when she realized she had left the scientists on their own. Would Lars follow her? Everything in her wanted to find Dwyn. The predicament was resolved when Lars emerged from the building and began his chase. Perhaps he had taken the time to secure his prisoners. Now he would be on her tail.

Having someone chase her almost felt natural to running. Sure, this person was more intelligent than her typical pursuers, but this one could tire. Audra's mind forgot someone was behind her, more encouraged by the possibility of what was in front of her. She knew what general direction Dwyn would head, to their more familiar and favorite running grounds. They would treat them as zombies and pull one of their tricks. Audra would bet anything that Dwyn was setting up for a Bait & Switch, but he might not know Lars was behind her. The configuration required Leap Frog. Would Dwyn figure it out?

Audra was ready to see this end. There was no way she would let them get the best of her again. They handled the zombies. They would handle these two thugs. Her mistakes reeled in her head – giving up Belinda, getting attacked by these two on I-16, letting Vesna be killed by Greenly's men, it had to stop. It would stop. She had given Lars a chance and he had refused to listen. The only way it would end was if Audra ran fast.

With Lars at her tail, she picked up speed, but not a sprint. The thugs were built to bully on even ground, but this was challenging terrain. She decided to catch up to Lindon and veer left. Her closeness would be too tempting for him, and he would go after her. This would allow Dwyn some distraction while he doubled back to come up from behind. That is, if Dwyn knew to do that.

It wasn't long before she caught up to Lindon.

"Hey! I'm about to pass you!" she jeered as loudly as she could.

She could see movement in the brush, of someone just out of sight. That must be Dwyn. He would be able to hear her. He would know her plan without a word of confirmation.

Lindon let out a slew of curse words, already tired from his current chase. He looked up ahead at his target who was getting away, then looked sideways to Audra. Her tease was just too much. He would make her pay for all of this inconvenience. Jobs were not supposed to be this hard. He changed directions.

"Oh, you think you'll get me? I'd like to see you try," Audra flirted.

She was flirting with danger though. It would only take one misstep in the root bundles to twist her ankle and have both men on top of her. She was playing with fire.

With the change in direction, Lars met up with Lindon and they ran as a pair.

"Where are you even going?!" shouted Lars. "There isn't a sanctuary in this whole world. We will get you."

Audra was impressed he could form full sentences behind her. She took a glance back. They didn't even have their weapons out. They were just going to manhandle her to the ground once they caught her. Audra knew it was perfect. She ran north, then northeast, before heading back around. She ran right under an outcropping of rock and felt a little dust and pebbles hit her shoulder, signaling he was in position. As the two thugs ran past the outcropping, Dwyn launched himself from above and fell on both.

As soon as she heard the thumps and crash, Audra turned around and sprinted back. Her knife in her hand, she was ready to come down on one of the two and end their lives at first physical touch. Audra arrived to see all three struggling. Even in the tussle, Audra could tell that Dwyn was not ready to take anyone's life. His moves were defensive and his cuts shallow and toward extremities. Audra reached in and kicked a head. It just made it angry.

Lars had managed his knife. He was close to Dwyn's neck while the other punched Dwyn hard. Audra launched herself and her knife sank into Lars's ribcage. He cried out in pain as Audra yanked it out and slashed for his partner. Lindon pulled back, but into Dwyn's arms. It was Dwyn who cried out as he made the gash along Lindon's neck, ending his life in a violent, pulsing gush.

Holding his side, Lars lunged again for Audra. Audra held out her knife in front and Lars stumbled onto it. Audra was not sure if he was disoriented or if the move was purposeful. He gasped a few breaths, whispered sorry to no one, and slipped away.

Dwyn shook. His whole body trembled in the excitement, the heaviness, and the distress. Audra cleaned her knife and put it away. She then took Dwyn's and cleaned his too. She put it in his side holster before pushing her arms underneath his to wrap him in a hug. He stood limply for a moment before draping his arms around her. She kept close contact for several minutes, trying to get his body to settle. When Audra thought it safe to proceed, she took him by the hand and they walked wordlessly toward the laboratory. They needed to make it there before dark and preferably before Dwyn went into shock. They had nothing out here and they had run quite a distance.

CHAPTER SIXTEEN

"They made it back! They're safe!" yelled out Ryder.

She was keeping watch from the front. Gordon came from the back of the property. The others rushed from the laboratory with crying and smiling and hugs all around.

"Where are the men?" asked Gordon.

"They weren't men. They were goons, and they refused to be anything else," addressed Audra.

"We had to… we…" tried Dwyn, who shook again.

"We killed them."

Satomi gave her a hug and whispered, "I'm sorry, thank you."

"They deserved it," sneered Ziv, "they killed Vesna."

No one agreed, and no one disagreed. It wasn't the outcome they had wanted, but it seemed to be the only acceptable one. They were alive. They had survived. A solemn calm washed over them. Ryder pushed the group inside. Satomi gave them food and turned on the kettle for some foraged tea of mostly dandelion. The entire team was wordless for the entire night. No one ventured to their rooms, but instead, they shared the lab again as their sleeping space. Eventually, bodies shut down despite brains reeling, and sleep overtook them.

Ryder was first to broach the topic in the morning.

"What will happen when the goons don't return to Lysent?"

"I don't imagine that the corporation will care where they are and why they haven't collected payment. But, they will send someone to check on the status of the laboratory. If we're still here, they will attack again. This time with trained people, not shamblers," said Audra.

It was important that they understand that the corporation was not going to forget about them.

Dwyn suggested options for the crew.

"The safest course of action would be to close up shop and move elsewhere. Otherwise, we tear up the place to make it look abandoned and hide out until the coast is clear. We could even hide a spot for you guys to do limited work while we wait for the checkup."

Ryder sat in silence. Her brain worked through the options, trying many simulations and perspectives. She then reported her findings.

"We can't move the things necessary. Some are fragile. The thermostat-controlled fridges are impossible to find replacements for, and too bulky to move. We need this place. We will have to convince the corporation it is destroyed, so when they arrive they do not set it on fire or smash it up more, but just go on their way."

"Who will stay?" she asked her friends.

Satomi said nothing but grabbed Ryder's hand to affirm.

"Of course I'm in," said Gordon.

He had nowhere else to go.

"I was here for Vesna," explained Ziv, "now she's gone…"

Audra expected to hear his opt out, but wasn't sure what his alternatives were.

"I guess I must carry on for her memory."

They all nodded in agreement. No one had any time to process that Vesna was gone, murdered, but they would keep going for her and to stop Lysent.

"We will have to break down the fence, burn down some of the buildings, and have zombies marching around. And we have to do it quick. When will the corporation expect Lars and company?" asked Dwyn.

"Lars and Lindon would have finished up yesterday, set up camp overnight, then made sure the stragglers wandered the opposite direction of the villages. They wouldn't push their horses to cover the ride back in one day. That would take them two. And then the corporation would give them at least one extra day before sending another couple of riders to check on us. I imagine they'll just take a day to get out here on fresh horses."

"Four days," said Gordon. "That should give us enough time to hide the valuables and destroy this place."

"After breakfast," claimed Ziv.

They worked together in glorious fashion destroying the laboratory. Gordon noted that everyone else had an eye for it. Satomi suggested it was all the destruction they had witnessed. When you realized what was essential, everything else faded away or in this case, could be smashed. Dwyn suggested that it was that Gordon may still be attached to things.

"I was still caught up on 'things' when others weren't. I was amazed at how little they survived with," Dwyn said as he dropped two Erlenmeyer flasks.

With the fence torn down, Audra and Dwyn gathered all the nearby zombies and placed them in the plaza area to roam around and make inspection difficult. It gave them a chance to speak alone.

"Hey, I want you to understand, I talked with Lars. They liked their jobs. They liked hurting us," Audra said.

"But did you talk to the one I..."

"These were the same thugs that hit us on I-16. They've been doing this for a while. You only did what you had to do," she said half convincing him and half convincing herself.

Dwyn had done what was necessary. He was always protecting the group. He had shown up at Lysent's plaza because he recognized their negotiations were too good to be true. Audra knew it too, but she hadn't discouraged Vesna. She'd cheered her on because it had a chance of benefiting her. Audra felt she had taken advantage of the group. And now Dwyn had to deal with the predicament her choices had caused.

Audra refocused her efforts on destruction. In a particularly brilliant move, Audra staged zombies poking out each building's windows, just itching to get out. That would create a sense of urgency. No one would want to be around when they broke free. They had fun burning an unused building, too. Anything to distract the coming scouts and themselves.

They minimized the number of temperature-controlled refrigerators and hid them away. If the lookout signaled someone was coming, they would cut the power to them. Audra hoped that the scouts would not scavenge their solar panels, but at least they could not carry them off same-day with the sheer number of zoms in the plaza.

With the place a mess, they packed up their supplies and left. Audra hoped they got the timeline correct and would not be out in the woods for long.

"It feels so sad to leave the place looking like this. It's like we were never here," said Satomi.

"That's the point," said Ziv gruffly.

The scientists longed for impact like Audra longed for Belinda. It was a worthier cause.

"You were – because I'm here," said Gordon, leaving the plaza for one of the first few times in several years.

They set up their tents a good distance away from the laboratory, and someone ventured back to keep watch. They used their tents from their travels to the laboratory, and now they had gotten to know each other more and were enjoying the time together in camp. It also left time for the scientists to consider what went wrong with Subject Four. At worst, nothing should have happened. Instead, the antiviral had killed the man. Ziv, who had created most of the process, was more defensive than helpful.

During a quiet moment during dinner, Audra broached their next decision.

"We need a new leader."

She still was not sure if she meant 'we' or 'you', but she knew the group would function better with a leading voice. They were all specialized, and someone needed to look up and make sure they were going in the right direction.

Ziv sat up taller. Audra rolled her eyes. He wanted leadership so he could order others into danger and stay out of it himself.

Satomi hesitated but then offered, "I nominate Dwyn. He is fair and doesn't seem to have a personal agenda."

Dwyn smiled at Satomi's compliment. "I fear I don't have enough experience," he said glancing at Ryder, "knowledge," glancing at Satomi and Gordon, "or skill," glancing at Audra, "to be your leader."

He continued.

"I nominate Ryder. She was the first person Vesna recruited. She has engineering and science knowledge, and she also has shown great leadership here at the laboratory."

"I'm just thankful to be along for the ride," said Gordon munching on his oat bar.

"That should be your election slogan: Take the Ryde," giggled Satomi.

They all let out a little noise before grief settled upon them again. The lightness seemed to remind them all they were choosing a new leader because theirs had fallen.

"Maybe you should hear what I think before you elect me. I don't agree with Vesna's plans. Greenly is murderous and Lysent has to go, but did you see those *zombies*?"

Audra had never heard that word come from any of the scientists' mouths. It was always *infected*, *sick*, or *subjects*. Never *zombie*.

"Those are the infected that Vesna wanted to awaken. Can you imagine their pain? They were in pieces."

Silence remained over the group. It was true. They were not viable people.

"Yes, it would topple the corporation, but at what cost? I think we should forget the aerosolization project. It's not working and I don't think it's what we want to do. We can talk about it, but none of us seemed as dedicated to that part of the plan as Vesna. We will still honor her, but we need to decide how we will continue our work."

* * *

Audra was on lookout duty, up high and tucked away, when

they came. She heard the crunching and clomping of horses and saw the movement in the woods on the other side of the laboratory. She pushed a button on the remote rigged by Ryder. It stopped the generator from turning on and alerting the riders that electricity still flowed. Audra used another relay device, built by their bored engineer, to alert the campsite crew.

Before the intruders reached the plaza fence, Dwyn had crawled up next to Audra. He did not want to wait at the campsite for news. They watched the two on horseback circle the plaza, gathering three or four zombies behind them. One horse kicked at a zom that got close to its rear. The commotion attracted more. Audra smiled. The more zombies they gathered, the more rushed their inspection would be. One rider gave the other his reins, and as they passed near a tree, the rider jumped off, out of sight. The zombies continued their path of following the horses. Dwyn gave her a little jab with his elbow, expressing that he was impressed with their moves. She was, too.

Once the tiny herd turned the corner, the dismounted rider approached the downed fence and stepped inside. Audra stifled a giggle as the man encountered a zom behind every door he opened. The man glanced into the laboratory and saw smashed flasks and things upturned. Another building was burned out. The man spent all of five minutes there before hightailing it out of the plaza with two zombies chasing him. He escaped when they got caught in the fence opening and tore at each other. At the sound of his whistle, his partner sped up in his lap around the plaza to meet him with his horse. The rider had lost all but one zombie. Audra was not even sure how. The man mounted up, and they left the way they had come.

Dwyn squeezed Audra's hand in celebration. Audra looked over with a warm smile before realizing they were sharing the same space. No longer in lookout mode, she could sense the warmth radiating off his body. Their faces close, Audra could see the curls of his hair sticking to his forehead.

Audra rolled out and left to notify the others.

* * *

"I knew Vesna before… all of this happened."

Ziv stood next to Vesna's memorial while everyone exchanged glances. Ziv always seemed so detached or at least reserved. It surprised them that he was speaking of her.

"Her husband, he got me this job at the laboratory, just a few weeks before all this happened.

"After, I didn't have much in terms of family around here, so Vesna took me in. She let me be a part of this. And even though I don't always agree with the way you all do things, I wish I could have given more to her. And I will stay here and find the courage to fight because she believed in me… in all of us."

With quiet tears, the rest shared their piece. And when there were no words left, the scientists returned to their laboratory and their work, leaving Audra and Dwyn in place. Dwyn gave her a light touch on the arm which seemed more for him than her. Despite having access to an antiviral, death seemed closer to them than ever before. He needed to know and touch life, to make sure it still existed. Audra did not respond. She did not want the touch to lead to a hug, to being wrapped in his arms. There was only one she was obliged to - and she was so far away.

The group was safe and doing well. She was proud of their pivot concerning the aerosolization. Audra's stubbornness and determination had sided with Vesna's direct confrontations, but she had seen where that had led them. And her desires isolated her from the others, no matter how much she cared for them. As her foot tapped the ground, her knife in its holster weighed heavy. It had been there for years, years she had been working for Lysent just like Lars. She needed to stop helping Lysent and instead, take care of her own.

That was what Vesna had done, even when her own took off with antivirals. The death hung close to Audra like a heavy tapestry she was trying to hold up. She was not sure how to help the group and help her sister. She needed to choose.

Dwyn was still at her side.

"You're thinking about leaving, aren't you?"

Audra wanted to say *no*. In truth, she wasn't sure, but in action, she had hidden her pack in the woods before the ceremony.

"I need to know she's alive, Dwyn."

Audra could not be sure of Rosie's words.

"And, I have to get her out of there by myself," she continued.

"Don't you understand that you are a part of this group? We can all work together to save your sister. You don't need to do it alone."

He was trying to persuade, but it confirmed her ideas. He was right. She was a part of this group. But she had one last thing to do, and it pressed on her heart.

"You can't help. None of you can," she said.

She marched to her bag and slung it onto her back before breaking into a jog. She could hear the thuds of Dwyn's feet on the ground, following her. For once, he caught her. He touched her arm, and she pulled away. He grabbed it more forcibly.

"Just stop, Audra!"

She punched him in the face. Hard.

"What the hell!" he said and then noticed that the girl was already in tears.

"I can't let you. I can't bring more thugs here. I can't risk you all - you're doing something good. And I'm - I'm doing something worthless but at great cost."

Dwyn's face screwed in confusion.

It was time to confess. It was time to give it up.

"She doesn't want to be saved… she never did," she spat out, remembering the last words.

Audra reached into the side pocket of her bag and handed Dwyn the ever-accessible letter. It had been in her pocket when Lars attacked months ago. She still had it to remind her, a letter her sister had written years ago. She walked off, disgusted that she would risk his life, Vesna's life, the scientists' lives for hers.

Audra,

I cannot do this anymore. I cannot walk around the woods, surrounded by the dead, hoping not to join their ranks. I cannot continue to rely on you, slow you down, and make you stumble. I do not want you to save me. I never did.

Take my supplies. I will not need them.

The falls are not far. Do you remember how much fun we had there? How our family was together? Laughing. Enjoying. Living.

Do not go there. I will be there, hanging from the uppermost bridge.

I want to spend my last moments where I have wanted to spend all my moments.

With love,
Belinda

With every rescue, Belinda had grown colder, angrier, and less grateful. Audra had believed if she took care of her a little longer, saved her another time, Belinda would get a handle on it and thrive. She just needed more time than others.

Dwyn read it over and for the second time, caught up with her.

"But, she got bit?" he asked, confused.

"She either got bit on the way there, got lost, or decided against hanging herself. She tied herself to a tree, not realizing there would be a cure. That she was not ending the burden, but increasing it with her infection.

"I just wanted her to be happy."

"Sounds like she couldn't be. And that's not your fault. That was never your fault."

The words cut into Audra. She had dared to repeat similar words to herself once or twice, but he spoke them with such certainty. For a years-old happenstance, it stung like a raw hurt. She retrieved the worn letter from his hand.

"I should have seen it coming. I protected her from death every day. We were surrounded by it and I didn't see it in her eyes. Death got to her anyway.

"Death is everywhere. I wanted to take this back from it. I will not let it keep taking from me.

"Vesna is gone! But YOU, YOU will stay safe! Satomi will stay safe. Ryder will stay safe. Because I'm leaving to finish this. You can't help me with this one. I need to do it on my own."

Audra took off on a run again. Dwyn tried to keep pace, but even without a pack, he could not keep up for the third time. He let her go.

CHAPTER SEVENTEEN

She saw it up ahead.

A glimmer of blue.

Not from the sky, but at eye level.

Audra drew closer, afraid of what she might see.

Blue flannel.

Her sister's shirt.

And there was her sister.

Her face washed and her lips stained with berries. Belinda's effort toward beauty was her signature, one lost at the end of the world. No one had time for beauty, art, or music over shelter, food, and survival. Well, that was not true. Belinda had time for them. Her blond hair was always combed and straight, occasionally oily when water was scarce. She whittled her figurines - robins and blue jays, a squirrel with a fluffy tail, once a whale with a waterspout. And when Belinda was not fearful, angry, or sad, she hummed throughout the campsite.

Her eyes were no longer blue.

They were gray.

Her skin was soft.

But it was gray.

Audra touched her skin and looked into her eyes and saw hauntingly nothing.

Belinda opened her mouth and reached toward Audra. And for a moment, Audra considered letting her.

She was all her sister had. And her sister was all she had. She had nothing now, but a broken promise to her mother. She dismissed her father's voice settling in the back of her mind. Belinda did not deserve this, no matter what her father said.

With a firm but gentle touch to not bruise her, Audra held each of Belinda's arms against her sides. She locked her elbows to keep distance. Belinda struggled a bit against her captor but remained calm. In these transformative hours, did Belinda still have some cognition to her? Would she be able to understand anything Audra was doing or saying?

"I'm sorry," Audra whispered.

Audra noticed Belinda's rope tied around her waist and looped around the thin pine they were standing underneath. Belinda had taken the time to restrain herself so she could not hurt others. With the rope secure, Audra backed off. Belinda remained calm, but still opened her jaw whenever her sister dared to move. Her groans frightened Audra. She hid behind another pine tree, her back against it. Audra stared into the woods. What was she going to do?

* * *

An unexpected visceral response accompanied her proximity to the Lysent plaza. The last time she was here Vesna was murdered, and Belinda almost died. At least, Audra was *told* she had escaped death. She had to be sure. A deep inhale and exhale lowered Audra's stressed shoulders away from her ears. She stepped onto company property.

"Hi Rosie," said Audra presenting herself to the receptionist.

"Audra!"

Rosie's eyes welled up and a smile Audra recognized from her mother warmed the woman's face. Audra knew it was true then. Rosie had saved Belinda from her stupidity and naivety. Audra opened her mouth to thank her but found no words.

"It's good to see you. You know we're under a six-month ban, right? You're often out for a while. I wasn't sure if you heard the news."

"Yes, I found out when I got back in town. Nasty business going on with a villager, right? I'd like to visit my sister, let her know it will be awhile longer before I earn enough."

Rosie smiled graciously and shuffled through paperwork. No one seemed perturbed by Audra's presence. They must not have known the identity of Vesna's companion.

"Just give me an hour to set it up. There aren't a lot of visits today."

Audra was escorted into a room like so many times before. She would sit on the pristine white pine chair and watch her sister until they asked her to leave. She had watched her for years, but now she understood. She was in pain, on fire, trapped in that body.

Belinda moved to the acrylic glass at the sight of her sister. Audra lured her out of sight of the door, to a section of acrylic with air holes drilled near the bottom.

"I'm sorry," she said for the millionth time.

It didn't begin to cover it, but she said it anyway.

She pulled out a syringe that Satomi had synthesized for this moment. Audra had made her promise to not tell anybody although she was sure she had told Ryder. Audra lay on her stomach and reached the syringe through the air hole, seeking the space between Belinda's toes. She injected slowly as to not excite Belinda and so it would not bruise. Belinda did not react at all. Her physical sensation seemed dulled by her illness and isolation.

Audra stood up and put her hand against the glass and apologized once more to her sister. She wished her sister would match her hand. She would soon if all went well, but for now, her gray eyes remained lost. Audra knocked on the door. Clyde came by and escorted her out.

"She was looking a little sallow. Could you have her checked out?"

"Of course, for a fee… since she's not scheduled for a checkup. We'll have Rosie set it up," he said.

"Thanks, and of course. It's like us going to the doctor… costs money."

"Yes, ma'am. There's Rosie. Enjoy your day."

"I'll come by tomorrow. I'm sure it's nothing, just want to be sure."

A few hours later, Audra watched two workers pull a cart out of the plaza and then outside fences. The body was buried, and the cart dragged unceremoniously back into Lysent.

Once they were gone, Audra began the furious but careful digging. She pulled out her sister, threw in some forest debris, and replaced the dirt so no one would notice. Audra put the body on a blanket and used it as a sled to pull her farther into the woods. She would wake up soon. Well, she would return from her coma state back into her zombie state, anyway.

Audra got her farther into the woods and set up her tent. She put Belinda inside with nothing for her to destroy when she came to. She made herself dinner and plans to run with Belinda in the morning, almost forgetting she would need to show face at Lysent to learn of her sister's fate. Would they believe her?

When Belinda emerged from unconsciousness, she did so with a frenzy. She thrashed about and yelled out as her senses were overwhelmed by uneven ground, warm temperatures, and concurrent sounds. She was no longer in her controlled environment and whatever old arrangement they had was lost. Audra gently gagged Belinda, laid her on her side, and bound her limbs. She covered her with blankets to dull her senses. It was not how she had imagined her sister's return. She left her writhing and took a long walk in the woods.

"Hi, Rosie. How did the doctor's appointment go for Belinda?" she asked.

Her nerves rattled underneath her skin, but her skin kept still and did not betray her.

"Dear, dear, come sit down in here. The doctor will come talk to you."

Audra was led into a side room. She put on a look of small concern and waited impatiently for the doctor. Just as Audra felt sure she'd been found out, an older female entered the room. She wore a white lab coat and small glasses. Audra stood up and shook her hand.

"Hi, Audra. I treated your sister yesterday. She fell in her room. You were right. She was sick. We do not know with what.

She died."

Audra did not say a word for a few moments, but sat back down in feigned shock. The doctor gave her a pat on her shoulder.

"Where is she?" Audra asked, her voice empty.

"We destroyed her body. I'm sorry. With the illness, we can't be sure it won't spread."

Audra gave a confused look at the lie. She recovered and mumbled understanding. She stared at her hands in her lap.

"Did her caretakers note any signs before then? When I saw her I knew right away. If only I had awakened her sooner…" she said half to herself.

"No, ma'am. Unfortunately, any signs she was ill were within normal limits in our observation notes. You must have a sister's intuition. There was nothing we could have done."

"I understand," she said.

She hesitated before her next question.

"What about my indenture contract? What happens now?"

"Front desk can answer those questions."

And with that opportunity, the woman excused herself and Rosie returned. She gave Audra a couple pats on the back before sitting down next to her.

"I'm so sorry dear. I remember when you first came here. You were too small and young to be a tagger, but you did it anyway. I'm sorry it didn't work out."

Rosie's eyes had questions. Had Audra killed her sister? Audra couldn't answer her here. She touched her hand in appreciation. Maybe one day.

"I understand you have questions about your indentured service?"

"Yes ma'am," she sniffled.

"Well, while you were in here, I was doing the math. The one million credits you need to awaken are, of course, not necessary anymore. Unfortunately, you still owe for rent, the two readers lost, and then, of course, the return of your current reader or the money equivalent.

"And also, we are charging rent for the six months no one can be awakened. Everyone is getting charged that to be fair."

"But Belinda is not here. You could put anyone in her cell. I mean, room."

"It's unlikely we will find another tenant until the ban is over. It's a fine everyone is receiving."

Audra could point out the flaws in that justification. She could argue that she had never lost a second reader. But, it was all academic. No matter what, it was more than she would ever see, much less afford. She just wanted to know the total.

"The total you owe the corporation is 1.2 million credits. 1.6 million if you can't bring back the reader."

Before Audra could react, Rosie continued.

"And since it's now all due, you will earn interest on the total as well."

Audra no longer had to fake her shock and despair. It didn't matter that they didn't have her loved one. They still had her in a financial vice grip and they did not expect her to leave the tagging program anytime soon. Rosie gave her a quick squeeze and told her to take her time as she exited the room.

Before Audra had time to wipe away her tears and collect herself, she heard someone enter the room from a different door.

"Ahem," came a throat-clear. Audra turned around to find Larange Greenly in the room. Audra stood up, not in deference, but to stand her ground. Greenly's guards stood menacingly large. She refused to acknowledge Greenly's desire to speak, but Greenly spoke anyway.

"I know you were in on that ridiculous negotiation with the traitor Vesna. You got her killed."

Greenly's eyes narrowed and she continued.

"And I know you killed your own sister, just to get out of helping Lysent and the villages. You think *I'm* the awful human being here? I've fed hundreds for hundreds of days. You've never done the same."

She devolved into yelling.

"Get out. Get out now! Don't you ever show your face in this township again."

It was a bonus that Audra's stunt had angered Greenly. Greenly *was* awful, so was Lars. The whole damned corporation was sour. Audra was happy to oblige the command for now. She gave Greenly a glare, turned heel, and retreated. But she would be back. One day, she would bring Greenly and Lysent to their knees.

CHAPTER EIGHTEEN

Audra couldn't stand to untie her sister's last surgeon's knot. Instead, she brought the camp to her. In her trek, she saw no signs of the infected responsible for her sister's fate. All of their supplies lay undisturbed and yet Audra felt as if she had nothing as she returned to her sister. And as darkness threatened to fall, Audra realized they had spent their first day in their new life.

Audra built a fire. Belinda reached for the visual and sensory stimuli without thought of self-preservation. The transformation was complete. Belinda was gone. Audra cooked and ate dinner in a daze. She periodically chided herself that she needed to figure what to do, but otherwise did not think about it at all. Audra set up her tent as close as possible, just out of Belinda's reach. She wanted to protect her from anything that might disturb her.

Audra awoke cold and reached for her sister before it all came flooding back. She ate out of habit, but little from lack of appetite. Her food supply was now plentiful. She found a good walking stick and rounded off the edges. She packed up her things and loosened Belinda's knot. She secured her sister's lead to her waist and guided her with the stick. They needed to remain on the move until they found something better. Belinda had always hated this plan, but now she followed without protest. Audra spun often to keep them from tangling on the brush. Belinda always gave a slow chase.

They walked an hour back to their earlier camp. When they arrived, Audra realized it was not where she wanted to be. She understood practicality would eventually win out over her grief. She would need a safe place to keep her sister or find the courage to put her down. But for now, she was moved to turn around. Her sister had wanted to visit the falls. And while that was where she had wanted to end her life, it was still a place of importance. She should see it one more time. Audra needed to see it one more time. She turned around and pulled out her compass.

The wooden signs marking the rules of the park stood tall but rotting. No one needed their warning anymore. A metal plaque gave information on the history of the falls. Probably important when the world came back to life, but survival now ruled. They approached the bottom of the falls and surprised someone bathing. He ran out and into the woods. By default, Audra hoped he was not part of a larger group that would return to change her plans. In truth, someone else controlling her destiny would have been welcomed. She would be free of choice, maybe even free of Belinda. She didn't dare think more.

Audra began the walk up the stairs she remembered from their vacation. Belinda could not coordinate the required movements. Every step tripped her up and put her on her shins and knees. Her face smashed into the stair edges. She tried to crawl, but still, it was too complicated for the diluted brain.

There were hundreds of steps.

Audra thought a moment and walked Belinda back to the signs. And yes, one marked an access road. Up the access road they went. It was covered in a couple years of leaves and fallen branches, but asphalted, so not overgrown.

When they reached the top, Audra tied Belinda to the bridge that went right over the falls. The moving water enticed Belinda, but the rope and railings kept her safe. Audra sat with her feet hanging over the edge and looked out. It was just a waterfall. Audra supposed it had been beautiful in a different lifetime. Not in this one. If she thought she would get closure here, she could not. She waited but found nothing. She still had a zombie sister tied to a rope, too many camp supplies, and nowhere to go. One of those issues was easily solved.

She pulled everything out onto the bridge and selected the things she needed. She left the rest in a pack for someone else to use. Then, they headed back down the access road. Audra had a fleeting thought of putting her pack on Belinda but changed her mind. Belinda was never good at carrying a pack. Why would she be now? Audra smiled for just a moment and continued their journey.

* * *

Even if she wanted to, they couldn't go back to the laboratory. Greenly had connected her to Vesna and the lab. The last she wanted to do was lead her back to the scientists' work. The first week of marching north was tough. It became clear that Belinda had been kept in tight confinement. Her muscles had atrophied and her motor skills had deteriorated. The stumbles were hard, but eventually, they fell back into old rhythm, just like the years when Audra had guided her after and before the bite.

Could Belinda survive in this world with just a little more time? With a little more help? Audra had not known how to help Belinda then, and she did not pretend to know now. But she had promised her mother. And she wanted to prove her father wrong. She was the last one hanging onto this rope. She had retrieved her sister and had hurt no one while doing so. And yet, peace still escaped her. It would come. Wouldn't it?

In the meantime, they would march. They would march for weeks. Audra wanted to take Belinda to a familiar place, even if she was sure that Belinda would not understand.

They took the access road up like they had done before. It was almost dark when they reached the top. And someone was already camped there.

"Finally beat you somewhere," came the familiar voice.

Audra said nothing as she busied herself tying Belinda to a sturdy tree. She was surprised that he had surmised her destination, annoyed he was there bothering her and her sister, and happy because she had missed him. She hated that he was there and yet, was glad to not be alone. The latter won out and after she finished her knot, she buried herself into a warm hug. She looked up into his face.

"It is good to see you, but I have other obligations."

She wanted to be clear that his appearance would not persuade her to rejoin the group.

"I came to give you this," he said as he offered a syringe from his bag.

An antidote.

Audra's eyes filled with questions. Dwyn answered them.

"A temperature-stable antidote. Turns out it's a lot easier to make them temperature-stable than to aerosolize them. At least, for Georgia's spring weather. Summer? Not so much, yet...

"I ran it here for you, and for her."

Audra fingered the syringe in her hand. Audra had worked hard, but all progress had been gained by her friends. Vesna had died trying to help a girl she never knew for a girl who had stolen from her. Satomi had made that syringe that had mimicked Belinda's death. And with another milestone achieved, a temperature-stable antidote, their first action had been to run a hundred miles to give it to someone who had abandoned them, to someone who after she received it, would have no reason to help them ever again.

"Thank you," was not enough, but the hug she slipped into and held was a start. She felt home. Dwyn gave his big, goofy smile and then settled into the hug. After a few long moments, she took his hand.

"I want you to meet someone…"

The river and falls below them seemed in perfect harmony with the insect noises around them. It was too late to give Belinda the antidote tonight. Audra slipped it into her bag, safely tucked away in towels. Dwyn had already eaten. Audra nibbled on a protein bar before she climbed into Dwyn's tent. She slept in her own bedding but curled up against Dwyn, who said nothing of the arrangement but rested his chin on the top of her head. They listened to the sound of the water and the slight shuffle of Belinda until they fell asleep.

The next morning, they woke up at the same time and left the tent together. Audra smiled at their spot near the river and walked with Dwyn over the footbridge to watch the falls.

"Something here lends itself to change, to rituals, to an awakening. It's magical," he murmured.

Audra gave a small smile as she hung her feet over the footbridge. Speaking of changes, she wanted to know what was going on with the group.

"We're scaling up our replication of the antidote. We've cured several other scientists, and they have been helping."

Dwyn hesitated before sharing the next part.

"They verified that there is pain during the infection."

Audra thought of Belinda at the campsite. She was in pain, and not just after the bite but before. Audra felt sure that waking her up to a world that was safe and civilized would relieve her pain, but maybe that wasn't true. And the world was not safe yet, anyway.

"We're going to undermine Lysent. We need help running, recruiting. I thought that the taggers who lost their loved ones would be interested in helping. Besides, if we succeed, many families will be looking for their loved ones. Tagging will be back in full force."

It sounded like a difficult world, but one she could help. It would get worse before it got better. Audra stood up and returned to camp. In the time that Belinda was gone, Audra had been angry, drunk, depressed. She had bargained her life in the process of making things right, but they were not hers to make right. Some things were out of her control. Some part of Audra knew that, but not the deep-down part.

When Audra turned the corner, she saw Belinda had pulled the blindfold off. She shifted her weight from one foot to the other in her excitement to see humans. Now whenever Audra saw the gray of Belinda's eyes, she saw the pain. She saw the suffering she had refused to acknowledge was so deep in Belinda. Belinda had made her choice to end her misery. She just had not known her torment would not end with a bite. Belinda was now helpless to the agony. Would waking her up end the pain? Or was Audra just refusing, year after year, to accept?

Audra turned her eyes away from her sister and toward the campsite and breakfast. After her meal, Audra sat for a long time staring at the fire, pleasantly warm in the cool morning. Dwyn did not ask her when she would inject her sister. He knew she would do it in her own time. She watched the fire die, from flames to embers, to no glow at all, just gray.

Audra picked up her pack and approached her sister's tree. She touched her face. Belinda pulled back and tried to bite the hand. Audra did not flinch. She reached into her bag for the antidote.

She arrived with something else.

"I love you," she whispered as she drove and withdrew the blade from her sister's temple with uninterrupted motion.

She reached out and caught the remainder as she crumpled, guiding her to the ground. She held her body and closed her gray eyes with a pass of her hand.

While a gasp may have escaped Dwyn, he did not say a word. He had come uninvited. He needed not invade anymore. With all his questions unanswered, he stepped away. Audra lay next to the body and caressed its face without attack until the sun began to sink opposite where it had arrived.

In that time Dwyn prepared a final spot in the woods aligned with the falls. After the silent burial at sunset, Audra sat by the grave and gazed out to the ever-moving water and the sun glimmering through the leaves until it was no more. She stayed for days and she mourned in a way she had never allowed herself. And Dwyn let her be.

When she opened her mouth to speak, she murmured partly to Dwyn and partly to the hushed noises of the waterfall.

"I feel like I've been running all of my life… away from zombies, away from death, away from accepting and mourning my sister's life and decisions. Belinda doesn't have to be in pain anymore. And neither do I."

And with that, she picked up her things and packed them away. They broke down camp and slung on their packs. It was time to move forward, to no longer meander through the woods focused on a dying mirage. Audra ran toward her group, to deliver antidotes, and to stop Lysent. She ran to awaken someone with the treasured vial stowed in her bag, toward a new life for the villages and for her. She ran toward herself.

ABOUT THE AUTHOR

RM Hamrick lives in Savannah, GA with her husband, two dogs, and a tortoise. She is an avid runner, currently training for the zombie apocalypse.

Sign up for updates at RMHamrick.com or follow on Facebook, Twitter, or Instagram.

67117558R00138

Made in the USA
Lexington, KY
02 September 2017